UNCLE AND HIS DETECTIVE

J. P. MARTIN

UNCLE
AND HIS
DETECTIVE

illustrated by Quentin Blake

Jonathan Cape
Thirty Bedford Square
London

FIRST PUBLISHED 1966
REPRINTED 1973, 1977
TEXT © 1966 BY J. P. MARTIN
ILLUSTRATIONS © 1966 BY JONATHAN CAPE LTD

JONATHAN CAPE LTD, 30 BEDFORD SQUARE, LONDON WCI

ISBN 0 224 61126 7

PRINTED IN GREAT BRITAIN BY
LOWE AND BRYDONE PRINTERS LIMITED, THETFORD, NORFOLK

CONTENTS

TO R. N. CURREY

who was the first
to introduce *Uncle*
to children outside my family

Some of the Characters

Uncle's Followers

The Old Monkey
The One-Armed Badger
Goodman
Butterskin Mute
Cloutman
Gubbins
Cowgill
Alonzo S. Whitebeard
The Respectable Horses
The King of the Badgers
Will Shudder
A. B. Fox
Benjamin Cheapman
Mr & Mrs Snowjuice
Waldovenison Smeare
Thomas Woeband
Colonel Lungy
Leominster
Tabby Bismuth
Ira Smoothy
Linseed
Heffo
Dr Lyre
Dearman
Malley

The Badfort Crowd

Beaver Hateman
Nailrod Hateman (Sen.)
Nailrod Hateman (Jun.)
Filljug Hateman
Sigismund Hateman
Flabskin
Hitmouse
Hootman
Jellytussle
The Wooden-Legged Donkey
Batty

Hated by Both Sides

Old Whitebeard

ONE

Badfort for Sale

ONE morning Uncle was sitting over his bucket of breakfast cocoa in the great hall of Homeward. He was in rather a dull state of mind. The Old Monkey and the cat Goodman were opening his letters, and every now and then gave him encouraging items of news. But it seemed impossible to cheer him up.

"Oh, sir," said the Old Monkey with shining eyes, "Sir Ben Bandit writes to say he is sending you a special herd of blue goats called Froddershams. They eat very little grass but soon get fat!"

Uncle sucked up a quart or so of cocoa, but said nothing.

After Uncle's great triumph over Beaver Hateman and the burning of Badfort, things had settled down to a state of quiet, steady prosperity. It was unfortunate that Badfort had not been entirely burnt out, but still stood, a shabby, smoke-begrimed pile, spoiling the view from hundreds of the windows of Uncle's vast castle. Still, the Badfort crowd did seem rather subdued. There had been no plots, no rebellions, no throwing of mud or stones, no smashing of windows. And the celebrations arranged by those who wished to honour Uncle had been staggering.

On one afternoon as many as twenty brass bands had been playing together the tune 'Glorious Uncle', while a hundred great drums beat out the time, and balloons mounted into the sky above the surging crowd.

In addition people from many distant lands sent gifts and deputations.

Six junks loaded with spices and dates had been sent to Homeward's nearest port by an Eastern potentate called Chan Kee Chunder whom Uncle had once entertained and shown his store of rice, a room about a hundred yards square and filled to the roof. He had sent with the junks a letter painted on silk, mentioning particularly Uncle's great work in supplying drinking fountains for the many thousands of dwarfs who inhabit the towers of Homeward.

A poem had also arrived from the Chinese sage, Mungo Rasp. It filled four books, and night after night Uncle had had it read to him by his faithful friend the Old Monkey or his cat Goodman. Will Shudder, the librarian, had a special compartment made for it in the library.

Most surprising, a deputation of small red-bearded men arrived from a colony established at the top of an enormous cliff called Whooshburg Precipice. They had heard of Uncle's good deeds, and felt they must come personally to thank him. The journey was so long that they were all exhausted and had to go into hospital for a while to recover. But they had refused to rest at all till they had offered to Uncle their greatest treasure, a small ebony image of Jorham Vinbusket, the founder of their tribe.

A Miss Venus Fodderburg had been so overpowered with excitement when she first saw Uncle that she had fallen at his feet and wept for hours.

Oh, it had been splendid, delightful, and then, strange to say, it all became rather boring. Uncle was glad, of course, that the Badfort crowd was so quiet and subdued, but at times he rather missed the attacks and criticizing of his degenerate neighbours. Of course he would not admit this, even to himself, but it was so.

"Sir, here's the biggest cheque for maize you've ever received!" said the Old Monkey, making another effort to cheer his master.

Uncle sighed so heavily that the cheque fluttered to the end of the table.

The Old Monkey opened another envelope, glanced at its contents and then put it aside. But Uncle saw this.

"Hand it over!" he said gruffly.

"Oh, sir, please don't read it!" begged the Old Monkey with tears in his eyes.

"I hope," said Uncle, "that I am strong enough for any kind of news."

The faithful creature handed the contents of the envelope to Uncle reluctantly. He always hates to worry his master.

"I'm afraid it's a cutting from the *Badfort News*, sir," he said.

Once Uncle had stopped publication of this disgraceful newspaper, the *Badfort News*, but it had managed to get going again. As always, it filled its pages with vile attacks against the inhabitants of Homeward. The editor is Beaver Hateman, and the chief reporter is, of course, the horrible little creature Hitmouse, who always carries a plentiful supply of skewers for sticking into people and who writes continually in a hating book.

Uncle's brow darkened as he looked at the cutting.

It was addressed, in red, to:

THE HUMBUG OF HOMEWARD

"Ha," said Uncle, "it's from that reptile Beaver Hateman, and he's up to his old foul game, writing in his own blood!"

Uncle took a deep angry breath and read:

SALE OF BADFORT

"Great woe has been caused to many well-wishers by the news that the vast, romantic castle of Badfort is for sale. It has long been the property of that excellent citizen Beaver Hateman Esq., B.A. —

"Pah!" said Uncle, snorting furiously. "Excellent citizen indeed!"

" — who, after a life-time of hard work and heroic attacks against the lying, boasting owner of Homeward, has been reduced by that same blackguard to poverty. Uncle, the tyrant and bully, deliberately set fire to Badfort. So fierce were the flames that at first it looked as if the whole building would be destroyed. However, by quick action on the part of Messrs Beaver, Filljug, Sigismund, Nailrod (Sen.), and Nailrod (Jun.) Hateman, the main part of the desirable residence was saved. Most of the rooms are still beautifully decorated and untouched by the flames —

"He does not add, I note," said Uncle, reaching for his cocoa bucket, "that most of the windows are smashed and the doors of these beautiful rooms were torn off for firewood long before the fire!"

"Oh, sir, this is nothing but lies," said the Old Monkey. "Don't read any more!"

"I shall read to the end!" said Uncle, picking up the cutting again.

"The Castle of Badfort is freehold, and through the beautifully laid-out grounds runs an excellent scob-fishing river. There is only one drawback, and, as we are always honest, we must state it. Badfort is overlooked by that castle of infamy,

Homeward, and the sight of that fat liar and traitor, Uncle, lounging by his moat must be frequently endured by any inhabitant of Badfort. Therefore our valuers and agents Messrs Jacky, Jacky, Varnish & Sogood advised us not to try for the real value of a hundred thousand pounds, but to offer the property for the astonishing bargain price of ten thousand pounds only. As competition for this property is bound to be keen in spite of the above-mentioned drawback, you are advised to apply at once to Messrs Jacky, Jacky, Varnish & Sogood, Vinegar Row, Badgertown."

Uncle smacked his trunk loudly on the table.

"Wheel up that two-hundredweight cake, will you?" he said to the Old Monkey. "I feel quite ill, and must have extra nourishment."

The Old Monkey hewed off a slab with an axe and staggered with it to Uncle.

"Good," said Uncle, "I need something sweet to take the taste of that scoundrel out of my mouth!"

The Old Monkey was delighted. His master had been eating very lightly for some time, and had seemed much depressed. Now he was feasting and snorting in the old style.

"Oh, sir," he said, "why don't *you* buy Badfort?"

"Buy Badfort?" Uncle looked at his friend in astonishment.

"Yes, sir. Then you would be rid of the Badfort crowd for ever!"

"Um." Uncle sounded thoughtful. "There is something in what you say. I could demolish the whole poisonous place, plant grass, clear the stream — "

"Have trees for swinging about in — " said the Old Monkey.

"A pond with lots of goldfish!" said the cat Goodman, chasing his tail.

"Oh, sir, it would benefit the whole neighbourhood!"

"Yes, a good park within easy reach of Badgertown is badly needed. I must speak to the King of Badgers about it!"

Uncle had hardly finished speaking before there was a knock on the front door. It was such a violent one that they all jumped. Another knock followed, so thunderous that it seemed as if the heavy panels must splinter.

"Go and see who this bad-mannered visitor is!" said Uncle.

The Old Monkey went, rather nervously, to open the door, and then turned to Uncle.

"Please, sir, it's Mr Hateman. Do you wish to see him?"

"No!" said Uncle. "I do not!"

But it was too late. Pushing the Old Monkey to one side, Beaver Hateman entered the room.

Uncle had not seen him since the fire at Badfort, but he was not changed. He had the same sack suit and hideous grin, and his voice as usual was loud, insolent and threatening.

"Still showing off, eh!" he said loudly as he walked up the hall.

He tried to snatch the cheque for maize that Uncle's heavy sigh had blown to the end of the table, but Uncle blew again. It fluttered out of Hateman's grasp, and was caught in mid-air by the cat Goodman.

"Control yourself!" said Uncle sternly. "Can't you even walk into a room without being jealous?"

"No, I can't," said Hateman, "and you'd be the same if you were in my shoes!"

"As you aren't wearing shoes that's a silly remark," replied Uncle.

The Old Monkey burst into delighted laughter, and this so infuriated Hateman that he lifted the stick he carried and ran at the Old Monkey with it. But the Old Monkey is pretty good at dodging people and he jumped nimbly aside so that Hateman's stick struck the wall panelling. It must have touched a secret knob or switch, for the panelling began to slide aside.

Like lightning Beaver Hateman hurled himself at the wall and pulled the panel back into place, turning to face Uncle with a hideous grin, humming a raucous tune in his flat voice, and trying to look as if nothing had happened.

"Thank you," said Uncle. "I know my castle has many secret passages, and you've just found what looks like the entrance to one I knew nothing about!"

"What me?" said Beaver Hateman. "You must need glasses! I didn't see any moving panel!"

"You lie!" said Uncle.

"Rot," said Beaver Hateman, twirling his stick and strolling to the door. "You're beginning to see things that aren't there. That's serious, you know. Well, what about Badfort? Are you going to make a bid for it? After all, the chief drawback, living opposite you, doesn't apply, does it?"

"To a person sunk in sin," said Uncle gravely, "the presence of a decent and well-meaning neighbour is no doubt a drawback, but, as these letters on the table show, there *are* worthy-minded men and women who would give anything to live near me!"

"Oh shut up!" shouted Hateman. "I know a lot of suckers are taken in by you, but I'm not one of them."

"Nothing but the thought that I might benefit these people would induce me to buy your wretched fortress, but in the circumstances I am considering the matter."

Hateman laughed hideously.

"Well, you can't have it," he shouted. "It's sold! It's sold, I say! That's what I came to tell you. Jimmy Linseed's the name of the man who's bought it. And he's agreed to all my terms. All of them. D'you want to know what they are?"

"No!" thundered Uncle.

"I'll just tell you one, then. He's getting Badfort cheap because he's agreed to take *me* in as a paying guest. So I'm in the money and still living opposite you to make your life a misery!"

A shadow came over Uncle's face and his ears drooped. Hateman swaggered to the door.

"That went home, didn't it?" said Hateman, laughing hideously.

And he was gone.

TWO

Malley's Tea-Room

UNCLE was very serious after Hateman had gone.

"This is bad news," he said. "Very bad. I thought we had settled with the Badfort crowd, but it seems I was too optimistic. I ought to warn this man Linseed about what kind of a lodger he's taking in at Badfort. Meanwhile, did you notice Beaver Hateman when he exposed the entrance to that secret passage?"

"He's got something to hide," said Goodman. "You could see that."

"We must find out where it leads," said Uncle.

"Oh yes, sir!" said the Old Monkey, who loves any kind of a change from housekeeping.

The cat Goodman was already standing on a chair and feeling with his front paws over the panels where the opening had appeared.

"I'm too big for this delicate work," said Uncle to the Old Monkey. "You have a go."

The Old Monkey has very small sensitive paws, but even he, pressing every inch of the panelling, could not make the wall move in the way it had when Beaver Hateman struck it with his stick.

"Look," said Uncle, "a violent blow opened that panel. Hand me a stone club and I'll take a run at it."

Uncle often uses stone clubs as walking sticks and usually has one about for use against enemies. So now Goodman dragged one across the floor to him and Uncle placed himself where Beaver Hateman had been when he ran at the Old Monkey.

"I'll stand where I was before," said the Old Monkey, "so it hits the same spot."

"All right," said Uncle, "but jump aside in time."

"Oh, I will, sir," said the Old Monkey, "but if you don't mind my saying so, sir, I would only strike the panelling a moderate blow. You are so much stronger than Beaver Hateman."

"A good suggestion," said Uncle, poising the club for a run.

As he thundered across the room, the Old Monkey leaped nimbly out of the way and the cat Goodman mewed with pleasure for there was a rumbling sound and the panelling slid aside.

"Oh splendid, sir!" cried the Old Monkey.

All three of them went to look inside the panelling. The first thing they saw, at the top of an immensely long flight of stone steps, was a notice saying: TO MALLEY'S TEA-ROOM.

"I'll never get the hang of this place of mine," said Uncle. "I thought there was a cellar underneath the dining-room!"

"Oh, there is, sir," said the Old Monkey, "but these steps must be built into the wall at one end."

"I've never heard of a free tea-room in my castle," said Uncle. "Get Will Shudder to look in that *A.B.C. Guide to Homeward* he's just found in the library. It might say something about it."

Will Shudder soon arrived with a tremendous book bound in black leather and trimmed with gold and red. It was so big that he had to wheel it on a book trolley. He was smiling brightly. He loves to be asked things. Once he worked for Professor Gandleweaver at the Fish-Frying Academy for hardly any money, but Uncle wanted somebody to catalogue and arrange the books in his library, so he gave the job to Shudder. He couldn't have chosen a better man.

"Nothing under M for Malley, sir," he said, briskly fluttering pages. "I'll look under T for Tea-Room."

"Who is this fellow Malley?" asked Uncle.

"Never heard of him, sir," said Goodman, who is very good at nosing out things.

"Ah – here it is, sir," said Shudder. "It is stated in the deeds of Homeward that a commodious free tea-room, with easy access to the people of Badgertown should be provided, and that an endowment fund has been set aside for this purpose."

"Free?" said Uncle. "I wonder. We'd better go and see how things are. Tell Cloutman and Gubbins I'd like them to come along."

Cloutman and Gubbins are two very close friends of Uncle. Gubbins can carry large weights with one hand. Cloutman can strike terrible blows with his large bony fists. Useful chaps when trouble is around.

"What about the One-Armed Badger, sir?" asked the Old Monkey.

Uncle looked round. Just behind his chair was a sort of oblong pile of parcels. It was the One-Armed Badger bowed to the ground with a pack of food and comforts for a journey. He is never so happy as when he is loaded with things he thinks his master may need on an exploring trip.

"As you're here you might as well come," said Uncle, "though we don't really need provisions or first-aid for such a short trip."

The One-Armed Badger gave a faint grunt of satisfaction and fell in behind the others.

"Now let's be off," said Uncle, squeezing through the aperture in the panelling with some difficulty.

Malley's Tea-Room was not as near as they expected it to be. First there was the long flight of steps, and then the passage went round and round and in and out like a maze, and at every turning there was a perch with a parrot on it. Every parrot screamed as they approached, "Malley's for good grub!" They had made about twenty turns and were getting sick of the parrots when they came into a large passage with two great ravens perched at the end of it. They croaked as Uncle's party tramped towards them, "Good free tea at Malley's!" As they croaked they flapped their wings.

"I hope we haven't got to pass twenty lots of ravens!" said Uncle rather crossly.

They didn't have to. Almost at once they saw ahead of them a door on which was printed FREE TEAS. By this door a crowd of dwarfs, wolves, goats and other creatures were milling about. Suddenly a little panel opened in the door and a big bushy moustache appeared.

"Be quiet, be patient," said a loud voice. "There is ample provision inside but so many people have come today that we need more tables. Soon you will be served."

Then the panel snapped to.

"That must be Malley," said Goodman.

Just then Uncle felt a paw on his foot, and looking down saw that the One-Armed Badger was holding out a large sandwich.

"Ah," said Uncle. "I'm glad you came – we might as well have a snack while we wait. A thermos of tea too! Good! Good! Sit down all of you."

Uncle's party made a little circle near the door. Round them gathered a mixed company of wolves, bears and dwarfs who watched every mouthful they took. Occasionally Uncle tossed one of them a sandwich, which was devoured with eager growls and scuffling. At last all the food was finished, and the One-

Armed Badger settled down for a happy sleep, his great mission accomplished.

Suddenly there was a loud shout and the tea-room door was opened.

By the time Uncle's party got inside most of the tables were full, but they managed to squeeze themselves round a small table near the platform where four thin wolves made a sort of singing group, accompanying themselves on tins and plates.

They were crooning in dismal tones:

> "Sometimes I'm very short of grub;
> My stomach will not rally;
> My pocket book is empty – quite;
> Then I remember Malley.

> "I walk into his tea-room vast,
> Sit down and order lunch;
> They tell me, 'You just wait a bit
> And *freely* you shall munch!'

> "Meat-pies and cakes come tumbling down;
> There is no bill or tally.
> They never say: 'You've got to pay!'
> They say, 'It's all on Malley!' "

"What d'you think of this place, sir?" Cloutman asked Uncle.

"I'm not sure yet, but the decorations are in first-class taste," said Uncle.

The vast room was painted red and decorated with statues of Uncle. One showed him opening the dwarf's drinking fountains, another on his traction engine (which he likes better than a car), and a third presenting a golden lamp to the King of the Badgers.

"I'm glad we've had something to eat ourselves, sir," said the Old Monkey. "There isn't anything to eat on the tables."

This dismal discovery brought a howl of dismay from every-body. Spoons were rattled, fists clenched and horrible threats uttered.

After the uproar had been going on for some time, Malley, who was a little man, absurdly fat, with large hands and feet, and a very small face garnished with a blackberry-bush of a moustache, ventured on to the platform. The wolf orchestra stopped playing.

"Good afternoon," he said, smiling rather nervously. "Some of you seem surprised that there is no food on the tables."

"We are!" said a sinister-looking white bear who had already broken two plates. "And if you don't bring some soon I mean to eat *you*."

Everybody shuddered, for he looked as if he meant it!

Malley's smile became so large that his face appeared to be breaking in two.

"Now, Mr Rufus Grizzly," he said, "we know you must have your little joke. I hope you've all noticed the little funnels above each table. When the orchestra begins to play 'Bliss Boy', buns, cakes and bread-and-butter will come sliding down these tubes. No charge, remember, you just tip the waiter. That's all."

There was silence at this. Most people looked fairly satisfied, for they were determined not to tip the waiter anyway.

Now the dismal moaning tune 'Bliss Boy' began, and a small shower of bread-and-butter and cakes fell from the funnels on to each table.

They were soon snapped up and then there was an uneasy pause.

"Any more?" shouted the white bear.

"No, no!" said Malley nervously. "But remember no bill, just a small tip to Mr Septimus."

At this moment a huge gorilla armed with a heavy wooden club began to move round the tables. If he got a tip he passed on, but if anybody hesitated he raised the club. The Old Monkey

actually saw him take sixpence from the pouch of a terrified badger.

"Der tip," he kept shouting, "der tip!"

In the end nearly everybody paid something.

Uncle was burning with indignation. This wrong to the weak was being done under his roof. It was too much.

"This must stop!" he said, trumpeting loudly. "I'll have no robbery done in my castle!"

"I'll soon settle this big guy!" snarled Septimus, lumbering at Uncle with his wooden club raised.

Luckily Uncle had brought a stone club to use as a walking stick, and now he calmly brandished it. Uncle's skill as a club-thrower is widely known, and Septimus suddenly saw whom he was up against and stopped.

"That's better," said Uncle, and turned to Malley. "I'm Uncle, the owner of this castle," he said. "Explain yourself. This is by

charter a free tea-room and you – through your bully of a waiter
– are robbing those who come to it."

"Well, sir," said Malley, bowing humbly, "I have such heavy
expenses – even apart from the food — the band, the waiter and
the rent — "

"Rent?" said Uncle. "I haven't received any rent."

"But I pay it every month – to a big rough chap in a sack suit
who says he is your agent. He's got large feet and doesn't wear
any shoes."

"Beaver Hateman!" said Uncle, his face taking on an expression
of intense severity. "I know the ruffian. You are not the first
person to be taken in by this arch impostor. Well, you have some
good points. Your tea-room is most tastefully decorated. The
statues are also well chosen, one might say they are uplifting. But
it is never right to force money from frightened people."

"Oh I know, sir, but I couldn't pay the wages without tips, sir!"

"This is what I propose," said Uncle. "I agree the original
endowment fund may leave you short as prices have risen so
much, so I will pay you and your staff a modest salary. I will send
you two chests of corned beef, two sacks of flour, and two kegs
of butter from my store each week, so that the meals supplied
can be more substantial."

"Oh, sir, what a glorious day this is!" Malley came forward
gushing.

"No fawning here!" said Uncle, halting him.

"Do I get proper wages now?" asked Septimus.

"Yes, but there must be no bullying," said Uncle. "Kindness
and politeness must be your watchword."

"There'll be no trouble, Big Boss," said Septimus, throwing his
club into a corner.

"Please, Mr Malley," said the leader of the wolf quartet, "what
about us?"

He really looked very thin, and so did the others.

"Proper wages will be paid from today," said Uncle.

The leader rushed back to his seat and all four were just about to plunge into a gay tune by way of thanks.

"Wait!" said Uncle. "So that a fresh start may be made I will supply the materials for a Founder's Feast. For this feast I will send you:

> "One hundred loaves of bread,
> Sixty tins of corned beef,
> Thirty pounds of butter,
> A hundredweight of apples,
> Six large gingerbread cakes."

Malley began to make a long speech of gratitude, but Uncle stopped him. He really can't bear long speeches of any kind.

"Thank you," he said, "no speech. The wolves can play a quartet if they like."

So they left for home followed by cheers and the strains of 'Bliss Boy'.

> "To see you walking down the street
> is bliss boy, bliss boy, bliss boy.
> To hear you crunching a large sweet
> is bliss boy, bliss boy, bliss boy."

"I don't think much of their songs," said Uncle. "I like a good rousing tune myself."

THREE

They Visit the Art Gallery

THAT night Uncle slept better than he had done for a long time. The dullness had lifted, and he had unmasked yet another piece of villainy by Beaver Hateman. Things were moving again.

Next morning he sat down cheerfully to consider his mail.

Uncle's letters always come in a barrel. Sometimes there are even two barrels and they are pulled steadily up the steps by a stalwart young mustang called Heffo. He had got the job of postman to Uncle after much competition.

Today he emptied the barrel on Uncle's table, and accepted the tin of warm mash that was always there waiting for him with a loud neigh of rapture.

"Sorry, sir, there's one letter you'll have to pay on," he said. "It comes from Sago Island and the postage is 4d. not 3d. You always has to pay double what's been forgot, sir. That's the rules!"

Uncle scanned the envelope.

"Very careless of somebody," he said, but he gave Heffo two pennies, which the postman deposited in a neat horsehair pouch that hung round his neck.

Before Uncle could open the letter there was a knock at the door and Alonzo S. Whitebeard came in. You will remember that Whitebeard is a celebrated miser who stays with Uncle as often as he can as it is cheaper than living at home. He seemed excited this morning, and when Uncle gave him a slice of bread-and-butter he quite forgot to stow it away under his beard – his usual hiding place – to eat afterwards.

"Oh, sir," he gasped, "Badfort is for sale and going very cheap. Although I'm a very poor man I thought I might try to buy it. There are so many rooms in it, you see. If I let them all I might make a profit."

"Calm yourself, Whitebeard," said Uncle. "I see no profit for anybody in owning Badfort."

"But sir," said Whitebeard, "I've worked out such a good scheme. First get the rooms repaired — "

"Whitebeard," said Uncle gently, "Badfort is already sold."

Whitebeard burst into tears.

"Don't give way to unmanly grief, Whitebeard," said Uncle. "You are well out of this, I say."

"But who bought it? Who?"

"A man called Linseed. And do you know why he got it? Because he agreed to take Beaver Hateman in and keep him."

Whitebeard brightened up a little, and then started to cry again.

"Pull yourself together, Whitebeard," said Uncle strongly. "This is weakness. You know you wouldn't like to have to provide four large meals a day for Beaver Hateman."

Whitebeard trembled violently.

"You seem to have had a shock," said Uncle. "Take this slice of bacon and eat it, man, eat it. And now you must turn your mind to other things, and so must I. I have my mail to attend to. There is a letter from Sago Island that looks specially interesting."

Uncle put on his horn-rimmed glasses and read the letter aloud.

"Dear Sir,

I take up my pen to write to you, though you may not remember me. Last time I saw you you were opening the Homeward Art Gallery. I can still see you, trunk in air, gloriously declaring the place open.

"Since then I have got on very well in business, and some people call me the Sago King. Therefore I have decided to send you £1,000 to be spent in any way you think fit to help the gallery. Long may you live to carry on your great work for Art.

Admiringly yours,
ROBERT TOADWELL"

Uncle looked round at everybody solemnly.

"This missive touches me deeply," he said. "I little thought an action of mine done years ago would bear such splendid fruit. Has anybody been to the Art Gallery recently?"

Nobody had.

"The least I can do," said Uncle, "is to go at once and see how things are and decide how this money can be spent. Does anybody remember how we get there?"

Nobody did.

Uncle's castle is so vast that to go almost anywhere in it beyond Uncle's own living quarters is a complicated business. And even after you've been it's never easy to remember the way you went.

"Call Will Shudder," said Uncle.

Again the *A.B.C. Guide to Homeward* was very useful and Will Shudder was soon reading out instructions for getting to the Art Gallery.

"Route 12996576. *Dining-Room to Art Gallery*.

"Enter cupboard at bottom of back stairs. Press bell – when

door opens proceed down Quack Walk to Crack House. Avoid door marked DANGER. Look for door in tower opposite Crack House. Straight on down passage."

"Sounds a long way," said Uncle. "We'd better take the One-Armed with some provisions. You, Goodman, had better stay and watch against enemies."

"Oh, sir, must I?" asked Goodman. "I'm so fond of books and all kinds of art!"

This was true. He spent a lot of time with Will Shudder in the library. He loves detective stories.

"All right," said Uncle. "I expect Beaver Hateman will be pretty busy hobnobbing with Linseed till the deeds of Badfort are signed. Let's start at once."

The back stairs at Homeward are not often used as they are so steep and dangerous. Great festoons of spider-webs hung from wall to wall, and there seemed to be a lot of smashed jugs at the bottom. All this made the going difficult. But at last they reached the cupboard. It was full of old overcoats and the heat was terrific. However they all crammed themselves in.

The Old Monkey pressed the bell and the door opened about a quarter of an inch only.

"That's not big enough for a dwarf to get through!" roared Uncle. "Press again."

They did, and the door opened another inch and then stopped. They did this several times and then Uncle lost his temper.

"If that door isn't opened at once I shall kick it open!"

As he shouted this the door opened so suddenly that they all fell out of the cupboard into an open space dotted with bushes between immense towers.

There was nobody to be seen.

After fuming for a while Uncle shouted, "March!" and they all

set off along Quack Walk. This was a little road which ran
between two pools of water. Each pool was crammed with ducks.
You could hardly see water for ducks and the path was thickly
scattered with eggs and feathers. The quacking was awful. The
ducks were alarmed at the sight of the party of strangers and the
din was almost unbearable.

"Push on," said Uncle, "push on!"

At last, to their great relief, they got to the end of Quack
Walk, and found themselves between soaring towers and looking
at a very strange old house. It was not part of a tower, but stood
by itself. It looked like a small castle with turrets and battlements
and pointed windows. The ancient door was studded with huge
nails and the word DANGER slashed across it in red. All this was
strange to see among a lot of skyscraper towers, but the strangest
thing of all was the extent to which the house was cracked. A
wide jagged crack ran from roof to foundations, and the whole

building looked most dangerous. It only seemed to be held together by great branches of ivy.

"What a very strange-looking place!" said Uncle. "I think I'll go and have a closer look at it."

"Oh, sir, remember the instructions said, 'Avoid door marked DANGER'," said the Old Monkey, who watches very closely over his master.

"At any rate we've come to see the Art Gallery," said Uncle. "We'll go there first and look at Crack House later."

"There's the Art Gallery door – painted yellow – at the bottom of the tower opposite," said Will Shudder.

There was a very small shabby notice on the yellow door: HOMEWARD ART GALLERY.

"Now at last we'll have a straight course," said Uncle.

Inside the door was a long corridor with a row of rooms on one side that were completely empty. At the end of the passage was a door of carved wood before which, set on an oak pedestal, was a small statue of Uncle.

"Good, but too small," said Uncle. "Knock on that door, Shudder, and let's hope we've got to the gallery at last. How can visitors be expected to go through all this in order to view the pictures!"

They knocked and there was a good deal of scuffling inside the door, but at last a key was turned and a small shabby man stood before them. He was wearing a cap with the words *William Snowjuice – Curator* printed on the band.

"Visitors!" he said, plainly astonished. "We haven't had any for weeks!"

"I am not surprised," said Uncle. "Surely, as the founder, I can be expected to pay an occasional visit of inspection."

"You haven't been at all since you opened it," said Snowjuice, "so it *is* a surprise!"

"Enough," said Uncle, for he was afraid of those endless arguments that so often pursue him during his journeys of discovery. "Let us see the gallery."

When they got in they found Mrs Snowjuice and six fairly neat children standing along the sides of the room.

"You and your family live here in the gallery?" asked Uncle, astonished.

"There's really nowhere else to live, sir, and that's a fact," said Snowjuice.

"What about all those empty rooms we passed on the way in?"

"You try and live in them," said Snowjuice, "you just try!"

"They looked pleasant airy rooms," said Uncle.

"But there's something wrong with them," said Snowjuice. "I won't have Mrs Snowjuice or the children frightened out of their wits."

"By what?" asked Uncle, getting impatient. He does like people to come to the point quickly.

Snowjuice looked round and then whispered:

"A great slimy fist – all draped in a sort of seaweed stuff – comes through the windows and tries to grab you!"

"Nonsense," said Uncle. "You mustn't imagine things, Snowjuice."

"Ask my wife!" said Snowjuice.

"It's true," said Mrs Snowjuice, nervously coming forward. "And you hear a screaming sound. Whatever it is can't get in here because there're no windows but only these roof lights. We've had to make little beds for the children under the statues, and I cook behind the big bronze group of Hercules and his friends at the end there, sir. It's not very convenient, sir."

"I should think not," said Uncle. "You know, Snowjuice, the only way to deal with something you're frightened of is to face it."

"That's all very well, sir," said Snowjuice, "but when it happens night after night you get kind of worn down."

"I know, I know," said Uncle, "but help is at hand. Meanwhile let us inspect the pictures. Tell us what you know of them as there doesn't seem to be a catalogue."

Snowjuice's voice was rusty from long disuse, so that when he began to describe the pictures he sounded like an old gramophone record being played with a worn-out needle.

"Picture 1. *Still Life. One melon on cracked plate*. Waldovenison Smeare. Early.

"Picture 2. *The Stolen Sandwich*. Waldovenison Smeare. Purple Period.

"Picture 3. *Breakfast at Homeward. The Owner of the Castle and Friends*. Waldovenison Smeare. Late.

"Picture 4. *Sunrise over Badfort*. J. von Jellytussle."

"That atrocious Jellytussle," said Uncle. "I didn't know he painted pictures!"

Jellytussle is a friend of Beaver Hateman. He looks nearly as big as Uncle, but he's thickly covered with jelly of a bluish colour, and his small glittering eyes are almost buried in jelly. He's a very spiteful character.

They all stopped in front of *Sunrise over Badfort*. It looked as if a can of brown paint had been poured into the frame to make a brown bulge. A small blob of yellow stuck out at the top.

"That's the picture artists always rave about," said Snowjuice, "when they manage to get here!"

"Well, I don't like it," said Uncle, turning away.

The other pictures were all of Uncle – opening the dwarfs' drinking fountains – crossing the moat – and opening the Hoof & Claw Trimming Stall. All quite good.

"But are these all?" asked Uncle.

"Well, a great scowling chap in a sack suit came with another

von Jellytussle. It was of you, sir, being hit on the head with a bottle of Black Tom. We didn't think it a suitable subject."

"I should think not," said Uncle firmly. "But I am puzzled about the lack of pictures. Surely there were more?"

"That's the lot, sir," said Snowjuice, "except for the new Smeare. He's working on that in an old shed at the back. He's made it into a sort of studio."

"Please, sir," said Goodman, "there was some mysterious writing at the bottom of the statue at the entrance. I think it's magic writing."

"Oh, that's Latin," said Snowjuice, "that doesn't mean anything."

"You're a good Latin scholar, aren't you, Shudder?" said Uncle.

"Moderate, sir, only moderate," said Shudder, who is a very modest man.

"Let's have a look at it," said Uncle.

So they all went back to the entrance.

"It's certainly not Latin, sir," said Shudder.

"It's just words written backwards," said Goodman, who was

able to get down close to the writing. "I had a lot of that front-to-back writing to read when I was working for Wizard Blenkinsop."

The notice read:

> Fi rof erom serutcip uoy hsiw
> nrut em ekil a hctiws.

"That's easy," said Goodman. "It means: If for more pictures you wish, turn me like a switch."

"Excellent," said Uncle.

He tried to turn the statue round. It would not move.

"Oh, not that way, sir," said Goodman. "A switch doesn't go round, sir. It never goes round. It goes up or down. Haven't you noticed that, sir?"

"You do talk a lot, Goodman," said Uncle. "However, let's try pressing the statue down."

He did, and at once there was a click, and in the wall beside them a sliding door rolled smoothly open.

They all walked through the opening in the wall and found themselves in a vast gallery hung with pictures. There must have been at least a hundred. The place was designed to be well lit from the ceiling, but the glass was so thickly covered with cobwebs that the light was almost too poor to see the pictures.

Uncle had a look at them. They were dull in colour and very stiff. Mostly they showed queer old rooms, very formal ladies and men in goldlaced suits. There were some of heavy brown rivers with barges on them.

Will Shudder gasped.

"Oh, sir, I believe these are valuable!" he said. "I can't be sure, but I'd like a second opinion!"

"Call Smeare," said Uncle to Snowjuice.

"I'll get him," said Snowjuice.

After a minute or two Waldovenison Smeare came hurrying in. He was very thin, with long hair and a thin straggly beard, and he was wearing paint-stained trousers and a coat made out of a worn hearthrug.

"I'll be glad to be of service," he said to Uncle, "but if there's an inspection of pictures I'm afraid I must charge a fee of fourpence, if you don't mind."

"Please give us your opinion of these pictures," said Uncle majestically, "and I will see you are suitably rewarded."

When Waldovenison Smeare saw the pictures he brightened up so much that even his thin nose shone.

"Why, that's a Jorvain!" he cried. "And as for these interiors, if they're not Van Hikkupers I'm a Dutchman!"

"Oh, sir!" cried Will Shudder. "I never thought I'd live to see a signed Van Hikkuper!"

"These are priceless!" shouted Smeare, waving his arms. "Worth a king's ransom! The *honour* of having them – think of it, think of it!"

Uncle stood for a time in deep thought. Then he said: "Has the One-Armed got the provisions ready?"

"Oh yes, sir," said the Old Monkey. "Two packs of a hundred ham sandwiches and a big bunch of bananas."

The One-Armed Badger hardly ever speaks, but now he said in a piping voice, "I put in an emergency ration of six tins of beef and six biscuits."

"Well done," said Uncle. "Let's have a spot of lunch."

They all sat down on a sort of octagon-shaped seat in the middle of the room, and the food was distributed. Soon everybody was happily munching.

At last Uncle spoke.

"Thank you, Smeare, for your guidance. By this morning's post I received an unexpected gift towards the upkeep of the gallery. I propose to spend it on improving conditions here."

"These pictures are suffering from neglect!" cried Smeare.

"You attend to them," said Uncle, "and I will pay you a salary for doing so."

"A salary?" cried Smeare, amazed. "Something regular coming in?"

"Certainly," said Uncle, "as long as you keep these valuable pictures in good shape. Now you, Snowjuice, have had a struggle, I can see, but you must make more of an effort to attract visitors. This gallery is supposed to be open to the public, you know, and you say yourself you haven't had any visitors for weeks."

"But the way here is so difficult, sir," cried Snowjuice. "You've got to be a very eager art student to face the difficulties, especially that wretch opposite!"

"What wretch opposite?" asked Uncle.

"Thomas Woeband, the caretaker of Crack House," said Snowjuice. "He attacks anybody who goes near. People think Crack House is a picturesque ruin, you see, and want to look at it."

"Thomas Woeband shall be dealt with," said Uncle, "on our

way home. Meanwhile here is a small cash bonus to help things along."

He drew from his pocket a handful of silver and divided it between Snowjuice and Waldovenison Smeare.

"I don't know how to thank you, sir," said Smeare, swallowing his last banana hastily, "but I'll paint your portrait for nothing if that's any good."

"Thanks, Smeare," said Uncle, "we'll see about that. Now, Snowjuice, about these rooms for your family, you say you can't get into them because of a being with a slimy fist who frightens you all?"

"That's right, sir," said Snowjuice. "I spent a lot of money on a bottle of magic stuff once, but it doesn't seem any good."

"Let's have a look at it," said Uncle.

Mrs Snowjuice rushed into the outer room and disappeared behind the statue of Hercules. She brought out a large flat bottle full of yellowish liquid. It had the words AGAINST WITCHES printed across it.

"That's one of Wizard Blenkinsop's spells," said Goodman. "It's good."

"D'you know how to use it?" said Snowjuice. "Perhaps I do something wrong."

"Do you say the word Nitram when you use it?" asked Goodman.

"No," said Snowjuice.

"Oh you *must* do that," said Goodman. "I learned that from Wizard Blenkinsop. You must sprinkle some of this liquid on the slimy fist when it is held through the window, and say Nitram as you do it."

"You can't do better than follow the cat's advice," said Uncle.

"But you can't go and sleep in one of those awful rooms, Willy!" wailed Mrs Snowjuice.

"Mrs Snowjuice," said Uncle, sternly, "you must be brave and help your husband to get rid of this trouble."

"And don't forget the word Nitram," said Goodman; "that's important."

The eldest of the Snowjuice children, who is hoping to get a scholarship to Dr Lyre's School in Lion Tower, wrote the word NITRAM down in his schoolboy's diary so they would be sure to get it right when the time came.

"Now," said Uncle, after they had left the Art Gallery, "let us have a look at Crack House. I'm not having any doors marked DANGER in my castle."

The rest of the party felt Crack House looked very strange and full of mystery with the great wide crack, almost big enough for a man to get into, running so crookedly down its face and hung with drooping ivy. They followed Uncle rather reluctantly.

As they came near to the ancient front door it suddenly flew open, and out dashed a fat frowning man in padded red clothes who pointed a large garden syringe at Uncle.

"You get off, you great skunk-hound!" he yelled. "If you stir one step nearer you'll get this syringe of poison full in your face!"

But Uncle had had enough. If people really behave badly Uncle gets behind them and kicks them up. Even the Badfort crowd behave better, for a while, after being kicked up.

Uncle shot out his trunk and seized the man by the collar. With one well-planted kick he sent him and his syringe up, up, up into the air. He rose, a strange red bloated object, much higher than the roof of Crack House.

"He's going to land in the pond, sir!" cried Goodman, excitedly running about. "Look, the ducks are getting out of his way."

It was true. Quacking atrociously, the ducks were all swimming hard for the banks.

"Leave him to flounder for a bit," said Uncle, after the big splash had taken place. "Then drag him out. We'll find out what his game is later. Now let's get home. I've had enough for today."

Although much had been done Uncle was uneasy about his visit to this old forgotten corner of his castle. Goodman was uneasy too. As they tramped up the long flight of stone steps to the dining-room he said:

"We've got to remember, sir, that even the best of Wizard Blenkinsop's spells don't last long. He'd never have any money coming in if they went on acting for ever. So we'll have to think of something else to deal with this creature who frightens the Snowjuices."

"Very true, Goodman," said Uncle. "I don't like mysteries that frighten people. This one has to be cleared up. But how? For the moment I confess myself baffled."

FOUR

Important Conversations

NEXT day Uncle sent for Cowgill, his engineer, and asked him to see that an opening was made in the wall near the bottom of the long flight of stairs which led to Crack House. At the same time he was to clear away any broken jugs and spider-webs and print a large notice:

TO HOMEWARD ART GALLERY
OLD MASTERS AND MODERN ART
ENTRANCE FREE

Uncle had no doubt that the ducks would quieten down when they got used to visitors, but he had still to deal with the door that only opened by inches. While he was wondering how to settle this mysterious and irritating matter, a letter arrived from Thomas Woeband. It was written quite neatly but was stained with water and mud:

Dear Sir,
   I feel I must ask you a favour. Can I come and see you at once? First, I owe you an apology. Second, there is *Something Going On* round here, and I would like your help in the absence of the owner of Crack House, Mr Ira Smoothy.
                                        Yours faithfully,
                                   THOMAS WOEBAND

P.S. That was a good kick. As I was wearing the padded clothes which are necessary at the moment it didn't hurt much, but the power behind it was terrific. I would like to serve you.

"Um," said Uncle. "I don't much like the tone of this letter, but on the other hand the more we can learn about Crack House the sooner the mystery will be solved. Who's willing to take a message to Woeband?"

"I am," said Gubbins. "I'm very fond of ducks. My father had a duck farm and I kinda like them to perch on my shoulders and quack in my ear."

"Then you go," said Uncle, "and remember if that door out of the cupboard doesn't open at once give it a good kick!"

Gubbins had hardly gone before Alonzo S. Whitebeard was shown in. He was looking very gloomy again.

"Now what's the matter?" asked Uncle, rather impatiently. He finds Whitebeard very trying sometimes.

"I've just met Mr Linseed, the new owner of Badfort," said Whitebeard, "and he says that Beaver Hateman is a most generous lodger. He bought a whole ham for breakfast this morning, and all he asked in return was for Nailrod Hateman to come and stay for a day or two. Linseed says at this rate he's going to *make* on the deal. He went singing and bouncing down the road. Oh, sir, what a bargain I've missed!"

"How many more times have I got to tell you, Whitebeard," said Uncle, "that anybody who takes Hateman as a lodger will regret it."

'And I know where he got that ham," said Goodman. "I was in Badgertown this morning and on my way back I saw Beaver Hateman take it from a Co-op van. He'd given the driver what he called a sweet, and almost at once he was snoring, slumped over the wheel. I expect he'd given him one of Gleamhound's Wake-You-Up tablets."

Gleamhound is a chemist who, with his assistant Eva, lives on the top of Homeward Tower. All his remedies are excellent, but you have to remember they work backwards or strange things are apt to happen to you.

"You see, Whitebeard," said Uncle, "soon the wretched Linseed will have the whole Badfort crowd to keep. Cheer up, you're well out of it!"

"I'll try to look on the bright side," said Whitebeard, sighing heavily.

"Please, sir," said Goodman, "about this Crack House mystery — "

"If you've any ideas let's have them," said Uncle.

"Well, I woke up in the middle of the night and I thought, yes, he might help us! The sooner I ask him the better. The only thing is he's very particular about what cases he takes and he may not want to do it. But I went to ask him, and I saw his secretary. And if you don't mind I won't say who he is — "

"Goodman," said Uncle, "sometimes you are a very wearisome talker. You must learn to be short and clear and not fog the mind."

"I'm sorry, sir," said Goodman, "but I can't tell you more in case he refuses to come and you're disappointed."

"I can't be disappointed if I don't know who he is," said Uncle.

At that moment Gubbins returned with Thomas Woeband whose red padded clothes were now dry, but much crinkled and dotted with dried feathers.

He bowed in a most respectful way to Uncle and asked if he could recite a few verses expressing his sorrow for his behaviour of the previous day.

"Please do," said Uncle, "provided there are not too many of them."

Uncle has so many poems to listen to that he gets very bored.

"There are twenty-nine verses and a chorus," said Woeband. "Is that too many?"

"Yes," said Uncle, "two will be enough."

Woeband folded his fat hands and put on a sad expression. Then he sang these words:

"My sorrow is frightful;
My grief is profound;
I slandered the master;
I called him 'skunk-hound'.

"His person is noble;
His deeds shine like gold;
The sum of his bounties
Can never be told.

"My sorrow is frightful;
My grief is profound ... "

"Enough," said Uncle. "Your repentance does you credit, and now let's finish with it."

Woeband looked depressed at having to stop so soon, but the Old Monkey asked for a copy of the other twenty-seven verses and the chorus, so that cheered him up.

"And now," said Uncle, "you say in your letter that a Mr Ira Smoothy owns Crack House. Where is he?"

"I don't rightly know, sir," said Woeband. "He sends my wages pretty regular, but he moves about a lot."

"And you are Mr Smoothy's caretaker?"

"Yes. I have orders from him to keep people away from Crack House. There's a lot of valuable and interesting things in Crack House, you know."

"What sort of things?" asked Uncle.

"Secret rooms and cabinets, sealed boxes that give you an electric shock if you try to open them, vases with long necks that pinch you if you put your hand in them, magic mirrors and washbasins. Oh, a whole lot of stuff!"

"Anything about Crack House in the *A.B.C. Guide to Homeward*, Shudder?" Uncle asked the librarian, who had just come in.

"A short note," said Shudder. "It's the oldest part of Homeward, and one of the few parts that don't belong to you, sir. Wizard Blenkinsop built the castle round it."

"I learn something new every day," said Uncle, turning to Woeband. "And now, Woeband, have you any idea why Mr Smoothy left Crack House?"

Thomas Woeband looked round fearfully and then lowered his voice.

"He couldn't bear living there any longer because of the THING what came to live in the crack!" he whispered hoarsely.

"Go on," said Uncle.

Goodman and the Old Monkey and Shudder came nearer so as not to miss a word.

"He said while IT was there he just couldn't abide Crack House."

"Oh sir, this must be the same creature that screams at night and scares Mr Snowjuice." cried Goodman.

"Exactly," said Uncle. "Have you seen it, Woeband?"

"Oh no," said Woeband, hastily, "I haven't seen it."

"You look a powerful man. Why don't you search out this nuisance and deal with it?"

"*Me* deal with it?" Woeband looked alarmed. "Oh, I couldn't do that, sir. That's why I'm wearing these padded clothes – in case of attack."

"I won't have any corner of my castle, whether it belongs to me or not, dominated by some nasty creature that everybody is afraid of," said Uncle. "I'm glad you've made your position clear, Woeband. When I first heard of you from Mr Snowjuice I thought you were working with this creature."

"Oh no, sir, never! If it wasn't for him, lurking in that there crack I could sit peaceful in the sun guarding Crack House and listening to the ducks."

"And syringeing innocent art-lovers who come to the gallery?"

"They thinks of Crack House as an ancient monument, sir. They comes up peering in the windows, trying doors and such. I have to protect Mr Smoothy's property. I told you that's what I'm there for."

"I'm sure Mr Smoothy never meant you to rush at people with a syringe."

"Well, to tell you the truth," said Woeband, "the job is getting me down. I just acts quick and then gets back under cover in case I'm attacked."

"I shall come and visit Crack House," said Uncle, "and you can show me round. After that I shall decide what course to take. Something will be done, you can be sure of that."

"Oh, thank you, sir," said Woeband. "I'd be that grateful."

"And no more syringeing," said Uncle. "If all goes well we hope to have many more visitors to the Art Gallery, and you must treat them politely."

"You'll never get any visitors while IT is there," said Woeband. "People know that there's something nasty at Crack House. Tabby Bismuth says you were the first people she'd had to open the door for in months."

"And who is Tabby Bismuth?" asked Uncle, sighing.

"She's the one who won't open the door. You see, she'll keep me for hours in that hot cupboard on my way back to Crack House."

"She will not!" roared Uncle. "Tabby Bismuth shall be dealt with at once!"

So they all went with Woeband down the back staircase. Cowgill and his helpers had already drilled a hole in the wall and let in some light and air. They had also loaded up all the broken jugs in a trailer attached to a traction engine and some of Cowgill's bird helpers were flying about brushing cobwebs down with their wings.

"Good work," said Uncle, and told the rest of the party, except the Old Monkey, to wait outside while he went into the cupboard and rang the bell.

This he did. As before, the door only opened an inch or two. Uncle went back for a run and there was a splintering sound and the door was open.

On the other side stood a tough-looking grey-haired woman staring with horror at a broken wooden bar. One part passed through a slot so that it could be pulled out a little at a time.

She shook her fist at Uncle and screamed, "You've spoilt all my fun! It's the only joy I have, listening to people sizzling and raging in that cupboard."

"Your name, madam," said Uncle, "is, I believe, Tabby Bismuth. Where do you live?"

"In that small hut, sir, and I mainly eat the miserberries from those bushes," she said, more or less politely.

"Well, from *now on*," said Uncle, "you will have a useful job to do; you will receive twopence a week to be my doorkeeper, and I want no more complaints about slow door-opening. Here is a week's wages in advance."

Tabby Bismuth did a sort of dance among the miserberry bushes and rushed back to Uncle.

"Oh, thank you, sir," she cried, "and please forgive me. Now what a glorious prospect is before me! On twopence a week I can shop at Cheapman's and live like a queen and have something over to give to my nine grandchildren when they come to see me. And there's a sale at Cheapman's tomorrow!" she added excitedly. "I may even get to that. Joy, joy, joy!"

"A sale at Cheapman's?" said Uncle. "Extraordinary! I don't see how that man can reduce things further!"

"Neither do I, sir," said the Old Monkey.

"Here's Mr Snowjuice running along Quack Walk," said Goodman. "Don't go yet, sir. I think he wants to speak to you. Doesn't he look happy!"

"What's come over him?" said Woeband. "He's usually such a miserable, timid sort of chap."

Snowjuice was bounding along Quack Walk, brushing ducks out of his path.

"It worked, sir, it worked!" he panted.

"Well, what happened?" asked Uncle.

"I took a camp bed into one of the empty rooms and lay down and tried to sleep," went on Snowjuice. "About midnight I heard screaming outside. Then that great slimy fist came crashing through the window-pane and started to grope about the room. I was shaking so much I could hardly unscrew the top of the bottle. Then the fist came nearer and somehow I managed to give it a sprinkling. At once there was an awful scream, and a hissing voice said: 'That fat elephant has put you up to this, but it won't make any difference!' "

"This really is abominable!" said Uncle, who hates being called fat.

"Did you shout Nitram?" asked Goodman.

"I'm just coming to that. I shouted Nitram, and there was dead silence. I was shaking from head to foot, sir. But suddenly the fist was gone! I heard the flapping of wings, sir, rising higher and higher. They got fainter and fainter, so I couldn't hear them at all. We'll sleep easy now, sir. I'll move the kids back today!"

"Wait a night or two," advised Uncle. "Such a creature may not be conquered at once."

But nothing would quench the high spirits of Woeband and Snowjuice.

"I'll give Crack House a good airing and as you promised you must come and see some of its tricks, sir," said Woeband eagerly. "I'm sure Mr Smoothy would want that after your great work in making the place fit to live in again."

"Caution," said Uncle, "caution and watchfulness, Woeband. Let me know instantly if the creature returns."

Woeband and Snowjuice went off arm-in-arm and chatting gaily along Quack Walk, kicking ducks out of the way as they went. The ducks set up a protest quack which made everybody in Uncle's party stop his ears till it died down.

"It's no good telling those two that the way is not clear yet," said Uncle, still looking at Woeband and Snowjuice.

"Oh no, sir," agreed Goodman, "and will you be in tonight, sir? I do hope so! *Somebody* may call. I'm counting on it! Oh, sir, I will be disappointed if he doesn't come."

"I will certainly be at home," said Uncle. "After such a day I think a game of spigots and early bed is all I am fit for. And I hope, after all your talk, of which I'm getting a little tired, that your mysterious friend will call, Goodman."

FIVE

The Arrival of A. B. Fox

AFTER the busy day it was splendid to have a good meal and the
prospect of a peaceful evening in the big hall.

Goodman was quietly reading a detective story. And very nice
he looked with his fur gleaming in the firelight, softly purring,
and giving a faint mew when he felt he was on the track of the
criminal.

All at once there was a knock on the front door. The Old
Monkey went to answer it and showed in a smart shrewd-looking
fox who gave a card to Uncle on which were printed the words:

A. B. FOX
Investigator

"Good evening, Mr Fox," said Uncle. "May I take it you are a
detective?"

Goodman was padding about excitedly.

"Oh, Mr Fox, I *am* glad you've come. I *did* hope.you would.
We *do* need you! I've often heard of you, of course, but never seen
you. I've never seen a real detective before!"

"Take your seat, Goodman," said Uncle sternly, "and keep
silence while we talk."

"That's a smart cat," said Fox. "What's this mystery he was
talking about to my secretary?"

"We have a baffling matter on hand," said Uncle, "and would
be glad of some clear-headed advice."

"I can help you," said Fox, "but my charges are high. Five
shillings a day and food, whether I find anything out or not. Even
for this short interview I am going to charge you half-a-crown.
But first I should like to prove to you that it is worth it. Stay
where you are, sir. Keep quite still. Don't look suspicious."

As Uncle was for the moment, he thought, clear of any likeli-
hood of attack from enemies, he was rather surprised at this
advice. However, he did as Fox suggested. Goodman and the

Old Monkey stayed frozen in their chairs too, only Goodman's eyes sparkling with excitement.

"Now," murmured Fox out of the side of his mouth, "keep looking at that window opposite. Watch me and watch the window."

Over the window was a small ventilation slot. While they watched, Fox slowly waved his beautiful golden brush behind him. There was a lightning movement of his right fore-paw, a sudden bang, and a loud squeal from the ventilator.

They all rushed to the window. It was not yet dark, and they saw the wretched dwarf Hitmouse flying through the air and landing on the edge of the moat. He was covered with ink and drawing-pins, and his hating book, without which he never travels, and in which he makes notes for the *Badfort News*, was floating on the waters of the moat. As they watched, he slowly swam out to fetch it. Shouting horrible words and pulling draw-ing-pins out of his hair, he went off at last towards Badfort.

"Now," said Fox briskly, "I think you'll admit that was pretty neat, and worth half-a-crown. I had my eye on that little scoundrel all the way from Badfort. I saw him sliding from bush to bush."

"Oh, sir, wasn't that wonderful?" cried Goodman. "I've never seen anything like it! Can I look at your gun, Mr Fox?"

"Just a pest-pistol," said Fox, modestly. "It explodes a shell containing ink and drawing-pins. Very effective."

"You're hired," said Uncle, giving him half-a-crown. "It's rather late to tell you everything tonight, but the full details of the Crack House mystery shall be put before you shortly."

"Right," said Fox. "Can your cat help? He strikes me as being a sharp fellow."

"He can," said Uncle, "as long as he carries out his daily duties for me."

"Oh thank you, thank you, sir!" Goodman jumped on to Fox's shoulder, purring loudly in his ear.

"Less of that excitement, Goodman," Uncle told him. "Remember the daily round first."

Fox then took his leave, and they all agreed that with his arrival things had begun to look better.

"Neatest thing I ever saw, sir!" said the Old Monkey. "The pest-pistol must have been hidden in his fur!"

"And the way he slowly moved his tail to and fro!" added Goodman. "That means danger. I know because I feel exactly the same myself. *My* tail moves slowly to and fro. I just can't help it."

"I must thank you, Goodman," said Uncle, "for getting this valuable helper. I feel relieved, I must say. To celebrate I vote we have an easy day tomorrow. What do you say?"

"Could we go and have a look at Cheapman's sale?" asked the Old Monkey. "It's a long time since we've been to Badgertown."

"As I said, I can't understand Cheapman having a sale," said Uncle. "Still if he is, and Mrs Bismuth seemed to know, it ought to be worth looking at."

Everybody thought it was a splendid idea. You can get things for next to nothing at Cheapman's. Motor-bikes cost only a halfpenny each, for instance. It means that all the other shops in the neighbourhood do pretty badly. Uncle doesn't do much shopping as he has such vast stores of everything at Homeward. When he does shop he goes to Dearman's, for the struggling little place would close altogether if it wasn't for Uncle's occasional visits.

"I don't think we ought to miss it!" cried the Old Monkey. "I'll take a penny or two of my savings!"

"I must say it would be good to have a day off for once," said Uncle.

"If only it was a sale of fish!" sighed Goodman.

"Well, let's have a bucket of Koolvat and then go to bed," said Uncle to the Old Monkey.

Koolvat is an excellent hot-weather beverage specially made for Uncle. It's rather like lemonade, but nicer. Sometimes it tastes of raspberries and sometimes of apricots, and you never quite know which it's going to be.

SIX

Cheapman's Sale

NEXT morning Uncle gave orders for the large traction engine to be prepared, and with two or three of his faithful friends and helpers he set out for Badgertown. Butterskin Mute, the farmer, had arrived just at the last minute, with a very fine assortment of fruit and vegetables, so Uncle had allowed him to come as a treat.

The engine went beautifully, and Uncle made a splendid figure as he sat on a gilded chair in the tender, wearing a purple dressing-gown, gold spectacles and a red-and-blue turban.

As they slowed down to go over the drawbridge, that horrible old man, Whitebeard's father, ran after the traction engine and swung on to the edge of the tender. He had tried to disguise himself as a young man and was wearing a sports coat and slacks. He had also dyed his grey hair yellow, and put a little whitewash on his bright red nose. It made him look even worse than usual.

Cloutman rapped on his fingers with a spanner, and he fell off, uttering such yells of hateful laughter that several perfectly green willow trees immediately turned yellow, and a couple of sleeping donkeys got to their feet and ran for their lives.

"We're well rid of him," said Uncle, "but look out as we go through the bushes."

They got through the bushes all right, which was good, as this is a place where Hateman and his friends often hide and try to throw things at Uncle and spoil his grandeur.

When they reached Cheapman's store they found it was impossible to get to the entrance. The pavement was crammed with screaming badgers, wolves, goats, bears and huge birds. The birds, unable to use their wings as nobody would allow it, were fixed tight.

A few animals had tried to practise the Old Monkey's trick of running lightly over the packed heads of the crowd, but if anybody attempted this he was immediately seized by the feet and dragged down.

Uncle and his friends were standing apart gazing with dismay at this sight, when a kindly grey-bearded man came up to them.

"I am Benjamin Cheapman, sir. Would you like to come round to the back – to my private entrance?"

Uncle looked at him with some curiosity. So this was the great Benjamin Cheapman! Except for Uncle he was quite the richest man in the land, far richer than the King of the Badgers who lives in a rather tumbledown palace on the edge of Badgertown.

Cloutman stayed to look after the traction engine, and Uncle and his party followed Cheapman down a narrow lane to a door marked 'Goods Entrance'. This was at once opened by a strong young wolf in porter's uniform, and they found themselves in a huge yard, full of lorries and bales of goods and packing cases all labelled with the name of Cheapman. From there Cheapman led them to his office, a large room furnished with gold-painted chairs and tables, and a magnificent gold desk with a chair behind it as big as a throne.

"I am very honoured to see you, sir," said Cheapman, "but I wish you had come on a happier occasion. I'm extremely worried, and really don't know what to do. You see I never have a sale — "

"But we heard of this sale ourselves yesterday," said Uncle, "from an employee of mine called Mrs Bismuth."

"Some villain must have started a rumour that I was having a sale!" cried Cheapman. "This morning when we opened the shop the people just swarmed in. We were helpless! I've sent for A. B. Fox, the famous detective, to see if he can find out how it happened, but meanwhile the people are packed so close I'm afraid we may have an accident, and my good name will have gone for ever! Can you help me?"

"I'll try willingly," said Uncle. "I can see the situation is serious!"

"I'd like you to have a general view of the store," said

Cheapman, "in case any solution occurs to you."

"But how can I?" said Uncle. "I am not fat, but I take up a great deal of room."

"Leave that to me. I'll just go and see if the air-car is ready," Cheapman told him. "Meanwhile, try some of these biscuits."

He handed Uncle a canister of large brown biscuits. Their flavour was excellent.

Cheapman soon came back and hurried them along a broad passage to where a sort of glass elevator-cage on wheels was waiting. There was ample room in it for Uncle and his party and Cheapman.

Cheapman's store is circular, and there are no steps but a kind of spiral walk rising gently from floor to floor. There is a great hollow space in the middle, with one gigantic pillar supporting the roof, and adorned with coloured lanterns. Round the edge of the galleries run the rails on which the air-car travels. In this Cheapman can go from top to bottom of his store, stop anywhere and keep a general eye on things.

Uncle was greatly taken with the air-car, and resolved to discuss with Cowgill the possibility of having such a car in one of the towers at Homeward.

They glided round and round and up and up. Uncle was appalled when he looked down.

The whole shop seemed one solid mass of faces. Here and there the horns of rams and goats stuck out, and one long-necked giraffe looked very lonely. Everybody was wedged tight. Those who were inside could not get out for all those outside were still pushing in, and the situation became worse and worse. A fat bear, clutching a halfpenny gown, had fainted, and had with great labour been extracted from the crowd and handed back, over people's heads, to the entrance. It was a terrifying sight.

As the car glided round, Uncle could see into the other shopping galleries. They were even worse than the bottom floor, for they had lower roofs and less air. The nearer the people were to the top, the more terrible was the crush. In the top gallery people were jammed together like pale wax images.

"What are we to do? What *are* we to do?" moaned Cheapman.

Uncle is a rapid thinker in emergencies.

"Have you a loud-speaker?" he asked.

"Yes, yes," said Cheapman, "an excellent system that can be heard inside the shop and out."

"Then get me back to your office quickly," said Uncle. "I've thought of a way to help."

Back in Cheapman's office Uncle strode to the telephone.

"Give me Number 1, extension 40."

"At once, sir," said the operator meekly.

"Is that you, Cowgill?" said Uncle. "Listen carefully. You know the emergency lorries that are kept filled in case of trouble? What have we got in them? Canned beef, loaves, biscuits and cheese? Good! Now listen carefully. Get everybody you can, and bring them and the lorries to Cheapman's store. There is big trouble here. Very big trouble indeed. You won't be able to get right up to the shop, but park the lorries as near the main entrance as possible, and be ready to hand out all the food. Right? Now look slippy, Cowgill."

Uncle turned from the telephone to Cheapman.

"As soon as I give the word," he said, "I want you to announce that there is going to be a *free distribution* of food outside the store, starting at once. You can mention my name if you think it will be an additional attraction. There will be a rush for the free food from places near the door, and this will relieve the pressure inside."

"Oh, sir," cried Cheapman, taking off his hat, "you are a wonder! You are a marvel! I shall never, never forget this. And now I will go at once to organize the loud-speakers."

As he went to the door A. B. Fox, wearing a pair of dark glasses, came in.

"Oh, sir," cried Goodman, "here's Mr Fox – and how well disguised!"

"Well, Fox," cried Cheapman, "have you found out how this started?"

Fox went over to Uncle, and held out his paw.

"Five bob, if you please, sir," he said.

Then he returned to Benjamin Cheapman, and gave him a crumpled leaflet.

"One of these pushed under every door in Badgertown in the last twenty-four hours," he said. "Printed at Badfort in office of *Badfort News*."

"Pah!" said Uncle.

The leaflet read as follows:

CHEAPMAN'S STORE. WEDNESDAY
VAST QUANTITIES OF STOLEN GOODS
AT HALF-PRICE. COME EARLY.

"Stolen goods!" cried Cheapman in anguish. "Lies, all lies! How can I live this down!"

"Idea behind this quite obvious," said Fox. "Looting of goods from store to start when confusion complete. Any moment now."

"This must be stopped!" said Uncle. "I only hope we are in time."

A. B. Fox, Goodman, Gubbins and Butterskin Mute went outside to be ready to help Cowgill the moment he arrived with the lorries. The Old Monkey stayed with Uncle in the office.

Soon a loud-speaker blared: "A free distribution of tinned meat, bread, cheese and biscuits, given by the generous master of Homeward, is now taking place outside the store. Join the queue at once if you don't want to get left out."

"Well put," said Uncle, and added, "I think if we station ourselves at the top of the lane we can keep an eye on things."

"Oh yes, sir," said the Old Monkey, who badly wanted to see what was going on.

Uncle's plan had already improved things. They saw at once five tough young bears, who had been fighting to get past a mule wedged in the entrance, suddenly turn round and rush for the food queue. A badger with ten small cubs, who had been trying to get them into the shop by passing them over people's heads, suddenly called her brood to her and made a rush across the road.

In ten minutes movement became possible in the store, and ambulance men were able to go in and bring out bruised would-be buyers and take them to Badgertown Hospital. One of these was a sow who seemed in a state of coma, but was still holding the object she had gone through so much to get, a small copper sty-scraper.

Cheapman came rushing down the lane to find Uncle. He had

tears of gratitude in his eyes.

"Oh, sir," he cried, "how can I thank you enough! If you had not taken command my store would have been ruined, my good name gone, my life's work all broken up!"

"Oh, that's all right," said Uncle. "I'm only too glad I was present. I must say Cowgill has organized the distribution of food splendidly."

Indeed the sight of the lorries drawn up on the other side of the road, each filled with white-wrapped parcels of food and silver tins, was a good one. Cowgill had brought his bird apprentices, as well as Will Shudder from the library, the dwarf Mig from the kitchen, and the One-Armed Badger. Even Whitebeard was handing over free food almost as quickly as the rest, but wincing a little from time to time because, being a miser, he found it hard to give so much away.

Uncle was not allowed to feel pleased for long.

"Just go and see who is causing the rowdyism at the head of that queue," he said to the Old Monkey.

The Old Monkey was back in a second or two.

"Oh, sir," he cried, "it's Beaver Hateman! He's walked right up to the head of the queue, and he's threatening the people behind him with a boar-spear!"

"The monstrous audacity, the colossal cheek of the man," said Uncle, "takes my breath away!"

Uncle handed his gold spectacles and turban to the Old Monkey and walked forward. His quiet powerful movement was like an army tank advancing over open country.

Hateman turned from the queue with his arms full of tins of corned beef and saw Uncle. Quick as lightning, he dodged behind the traction engine, and leered out from the side of the big wheel.

"Ha, ha!" he yelled. "Bully Bounty is here, is he? Thank you for the load of free grub, you boaster and blackguard!"

He dashed off down a side street.

The Old Monkey was nearly crying and so was Benjamin Cheapman.

"That this should happen after all you've done!" moaned Cheapman.

"He shall still not go unpunished," said Uncle, breathing heavily. "He may have escaped me this time, but he will suffer for today's work – and soon!"

"Please come with me to the office," begged Cheapman. "Forget this degraded incident, and give me the pleasure of expressing my gratitude to you with a small gift."

He took Uncle and the Old Monkey back to his office and from his safe produced a beautiful pair of elephant's boots encrusted with rubies and emeralds.

"These," he said, "were given to my father for saving the life of some rajah. Not being an elephant, he was not able to wear them, but he put them away. They are now yours. You have saved, if not my life, my reputation, and this is dearer to me than life. Accept them, I beseech you, and when you put them on remember my gratitude."

Uncle was too moved to speak, but he grasped Cheapman's hand and the magnate well understood.

As they were going back to the traction engine they passed Dearman's store. This dealer puts his prices up every day, and he was, at this moment, pinning up a ticket on an elephant's mackintosh. The ticket read:

> YESTERDAY'S PRICE £532 10s. 6d.
> TODAY'S PRICE £50

Uncle went in.

"Oh, sir, it's you!" cried Dearman, wiping away his tears. "To think you should have remembered me while such an attractive sale was going on!"

"Here are fifty pounds," said Uncle. "Take down the mack and give it to the Old Monkey, and we must then be on our way."

"Oh happy day!" cried Dearman, but Uncle did not wait to hear more. He was tired and wanted to get home.

SEVEN

Morning by the Moat

THEY stayed at home for a day or two after Cheapman's sale, for they all needed a rest and time to forget the ignominious incident which had clouded the day.

The weather was splendid and they had a good many swims in the moat.

Uncle was going through his papers. He was thinking of writing his life, and Will Shudder had offered to take down his reminiscences in shorthand and turn them into a first-class book.

One fine morning as they sat by the moat Uncle decided to start dictating. There was a whole stem of bananas, which means about a hundred bananas, on the table before them and a large tub of Koolvat.

In the afternoon they had all been invited to return to Crack House to see some of its wonders. There had been no word from Woeband that the creature had tried to get back into the crack, but all the same Uncle had asked A. B. Fox to go and see what he could make of the situation. He offered to send one or two people with him, but Fox said he would like to go by himself.

"Independent fellow, this chap Fox," said Uncle.

It looked like being a peaceful morning.

"Are you ready, sir?" asked Shudder, his pencil poised over his notebook.

Uncle cleared his throat. It's never easy to start a book, but finally he began to dictate.

"This is the story of my life. I was born in the depths of the jungle of poor but honest parents, and thrust out into the world at a tender age. Alone, weak, ignorant, all the capital I had was one halfpenny — "

Shudder was finding it hard to keep up. "What came after 'Alone, weak and ignorant', sir?" he asked.

At that moment the Old Monkey appeared, leading a small man who was a stranger to Uncle.

"Really!" said Uncle, annoyed. "Is there no peace in this place? Writing a book is difficult work, and I was just getting into my stride."

"Please sir," said the Old Money, "this is Mr Linseed and he is most anxious to see you."

Curiosity made Uncle forget his annoyance. So this anxious and trembling man was the new owner of Badfort! He looked, with his carefully smoothed-down black hair, neat moustache, and trim dark suit, as if he would naturally be cheerful and sure of himself, but he was far from being that now.

"Good morning, sir," he said in a low shaky voice. "I would much appreciate a short talk with you in private."

Uncle told the others to go and have a swim in the moat.

"Take the bananas with you," he said, and added: "No, leave twenty or so on the table. Have a banana, Linseed."

"Thank you, sir," said Linseed in a listless voice. "It may help me to talk."

"I gather you are in difficulties over your purchase of Badfort," said Uncle when they were alone.

"Indeed yes," said Linseed, "and I started off with such high hopes. But the trouble is the place is no longer my own."

"I can't say I'm surprised!" said Uncle.

Linseed seemed unable to go on but Uncle handed him a cup of Koolvat and after drinking it he managed to speak in a trembling furious voice.

"D'you know how many people I had sitting down to breakfast in Badfort this morning? Ten of them, ten, and all with the appetites of wolves, and none of them friends of mine! There's one greedy little creature called Hitmouse who lives in a hut near the gate, but he comes to all meals, and once when I objected he stuck a skewer into me!"

"Sad, sad!" said Uncle, pouring out more Koolvat for them both.

"And there's a monster called Flabskin who eats very slowly and stops at the table from breakfast till dinner, chewing all the time and making the most awful faces. And there's another one even worse than him. He's huge and made of jelly of a bluish colour."

"Jellytussle," said Uncle. "I am sorry to say I know him well."

"It's fetch and carry, fetch and carry all day long. If I object, Hateman says the host always serves and provides the food. And he sits there grinning with his feet on the table."

"Atrocious!" said Uncle.

"I've spent all the money I made in business," wailed Linseed, "on buying Badfort!"

"What was your business?" asked Uncle.

"Mainly grocery, but I had one or two fancy side-lines. My spiced red-onion bar did splendidly, but where I really made money was in police snacks."

"And what are police snacks?" asked Uncle.

"Little nourishing sandwiches for policemen on the beat. Oh, I coined money with those! Policemen are always hungry, you see, and the sandwiches were small but very filling. They could just pop one in every time they passed the stall, and yet never appear to be eating on duty."

"A good and enterprising notion," said Uncle, "and I only wish I could say the same about your purchase of Badfort."

Linseed sobbed.

"I was going to let all the rooms and have a peaceful life just collecting rents."

"If you had come to me before you bought the place," said Uncle, "I would have told you what scorpions you were dealing with."

"Beaver Hateman said awful things about you too," said Linseed, "and I am afraid I was silly enough to believe him."

"Silly is the right word," said Uncle, "but say no more, you have suffered enough. You have the deeds of Badfort?"

"Yes," said Linseed, "I signed those, of course."

"Well, the place still belongs to you, but my advice is to get what money you can from Beaver Hateman and clear out."

"Clear out?" cried Linseed, in anguish.

"Only thing to do," said Uncle, "and come to me if you need further advice."

Sighing heavily, Linseed went away. He paused on the draw-bridge to watch with envious eyes the carefree splashing of Uncle's followers in the water below.

Will Shudder came back with his notebook, eager to get on with Uncle's autobiography.

"As we've been so much interrupted, Shudder," said Uncle, "I think we'll have an early lunch and get to Crack House in good time. At any rate we've made a start on the book."

Will Shudder agreed that they had, but he looked rather disappointed.

EIGHT

Crack House

ALONZO S. WHITEBEARD was to be allowed to come on the visit to Crack House as he had behaved generously – for him – over the hand-out at Cheapman's store. Cloutman and Gubbins could not come as they were mowing a lawn a mile square on the north side of Homeward. Will Shudder and the One-Armed Badger came instead.

When they got to the bottom of the staircase, which was now cleaned and well lit, they rang the bell in the cupboard and the door was at once smoothly opened. A changed Tabby Bismuth stood before them.

She was wearing a neat pink dress and new shoes, and was munching an apple tart.

"I'm glad to see this big improvement in you," said Uncle.

"Oh, what a week I've had!" cried Tabby Bismuth. "Not a miserberry have I had to eat."

"Now we must press on," said Uncle. "Always open the door smartly, Mrs Bismuth, and I shall be satisfied."

This time the ducks were much quieter. They seemed so docile and friendly that Whitebeard captured one and tried to hide it under his beard, having visions of a hot duck for supper. The duck nearly bit a piece out of his chest, and with a roar of pain Whitebeard flung it from him. Everybody laughed.

"You were rather too sharp that time, Whitebeard," said Uncle.

When they got to Crack House they were pleased to see most of the windows had been cleaned, and the whole place looked more cheerful. Of course the crack was still there and made it continue to look sinister. There was nothing in the crack now, as far as a quick look under the cascade of ivy could reveal, but they noticed a peculiar musty smell. Uncle thought he had smelt it before in old buildings.

Woeband, looking half the size without his red padded clothes, and wearing a porter's apron, opened the door.

"Welcome to Crack House, sir," he said.

"Thanks, Woeband," said Uncle. "How are things?"

"Everything shipshape and easy," said Woeband. "All quiet at nights, and Mrs Snowjuice has been putting up flowered curtains at the windows opposite. Very select the neighbourhood is getting, sir."

"Good, good," said Uncle. "Long may it last!"

"Come into the dining-room, sir," said Woeband.

He led them into a big stately room with a floor tiled in blue and yellow in a very complicated pattern. There was a very good table with massive carved legs in the middle of the room, and a number of carved chairs. Nothing else much. The walls seemed to be of glass, and in the one opposite to the door through which Uncle and his party entered was an archway leading to a long corridor.

"If you wouldn't mind going under the archway and into the corridor opposite," said Woeband respectfully to Uncle, "there is something very interesting for you to see, sir."

"Certainly. We are here to see what we can," said Uncle and tramped across the room to the archway.

Bang! His massive forehead crashed into a solid glass wall just as he was expecting to go through the archway.

"Oh sir!" gasped the Old Monkey. "You aren't hurt, are you?"

"No!" roared Uncle, and then turned to Woeband. "This is a nice way to treat visitors."

Woeband was laughing so much that he could hardly stand.

"Mr Smoothy had these walls made specially to catch thieves," he said. "It's all done by springs. See, there's a corridor and an archway in each wall. It's very baffling. Thieves rush about in here banging themselves, and then fall down flat and are at your mercy."

"Very ingenious and useful," said Uncle, crossly, "but hardly the thing to try out on guests."

Uncle doesn't often have tricks played on him in this way, and he little thought, as he rubbed his forehead, that this particular one was to be a great help in a future desperate battle.

"I'm sorry, sir," said Woeband, trying to stop laughing, "but there's no other way to show you. Telling you's no good. You've got to *feel* it."

"Well, I have done," said Uncle. "Is there anything else of interest?"

"You all look pretty grimy," said Woeband. "Wouldn't you like a wash?"

"That again is not the sort of thing to say to guests, Woeband," said Uncle, "but perhaps we could do with a rinse after our walk."

Woeband led the way to an attractive-looking bathroom painted blue. There was a large washbasin, but no taps.

71

"You just pull the plug out," said Woeband, smiling broadly, "and the water comes up."

"Ah, this *is* a novelty," said Uncle. "I see now why you were in such a hurry to get us into the bathroom."

They all tried the bowl and it worked splendidly. When you wanted to empty it you just replaced the plug and the water ran out.

"This and the bath are two of Mr Smoothy's jokes for visitors," said Woeband, rubbing his hands with pleasure.

"I don't see any bath," said Uncle, looking round.

"Well, you see that bath mat on the floor, sir," said Woeband, eagerly. "You just lies on that and presses that switch."

"You lie on it," said Uncle to the Old Monkey. ' You haven't got many clothes on."

The Old Monkey lay down on the bath mat, put out his paw and pressed the switch.

At once the sides of a large blue bath began to rise out of some narrow slits that seemed part of the design of the tiled floor, and the bath filled with water as it rose. In less than ten seconds it had risen to the height of three feet and the Old Monkey was floating happily in beautifully warm water.

"Just press the switch again," said Woeband, "and you'll find yourself lying on the mat."

The Old Monkey did so and the bath and the water silently disappeared.

"Now give yourself a good rub down," said Woeband, handing the Old Monkey a rough towel.

"I like this bath immensely," said Uncle, "but I'm afraid I'd be too big for it."

"Oh no, sir," said Woeband, "if you decided to use it you'd find it was big enough. Would you like to try?"

"Another day," said Uncle, who likes bathing but likes novelties even better. "What else is there to see?"

"Let me show you Mr Smoothy's kitchen," was the reply.

Woeband led them into a square room with nothing in it but wall cupboards and a small box in the middle of the floor.

"Now you see that box," said Woeband. "It's filled with a gallon of thousand-year oil. You can see it through this little door."

He pushed aside a panel and they all saw a dim green flame.

"Put anything in these cupboards," said Woeband, "and it cooks at once. Anybody got a raw steak?"

"What a thing to ask!" said Uncle.

But surprisingly the One-Armed Badger had one in his bundle, and handed it over on a tin plate.

"Right," said Woeband, "I takes this 'ere steak, puts it in this cupboard on a plate. Shut the door. Take an oven cloth. Open the door. There you are, sir!"

And Woeband showed Uncle a perfectly cooked steak.

"Well," said Uncle, "this is a big improvement on the oxy-acetylene cooker Mig uses in my kitchen. I must inquire into this."

"That's thousand-year oil for you," said Woeband proudly. "I've never known Mr Smoothy have more than the one gallon. It lasts for years. And now let me show you the study."

The study was small compared with Uncle's library, of course, and was much more ordinary to look at. The most remarkable thing about it was that it had books on the ceiling.

Will Shudder was much struck by this, and he gasped when he saw what appeared to be a very charming inlaid ceiling made entirely of books.

"But how do they stay up and how does he get them down?" he cried.

"Well, he doesn't read much," said Woeband, "but if he wants to he just pulls one of them cords, all lettered from A to Z, and the bookshelf comes down and settles on the desk."

They saw now that there were some gold cords attached to holders on the walls. Woeband pulled one, and a shelf of books moved out of the ceiling on a sort of expanding metal arm and came quietly to rest on the desk. All the books were fixed on the shelves by strong metal clips.

"Mr Smoothy got so short of space; that's why he hit on this idea," said Woeband. "This is Mr Smoothy's desk."

Uncle sat down at it. The chair was so big that he felt quite comfortable in it. There were a lot of interesting things on the desk in front of him. An inkstand shaped like a badger, and some paper clips almost as big as handcuffs. But what really caught Uncle's eye was a row of small books bound in gilt. Each one had the same title, *Golden Sayings of Uncle*.

"Ah," said Uncle, "this Mr Smoothy must be a remarkable character."

"Oh he is, sir," said Woeband, "a very joky clever gentleman."

"I think I might look in those volumes," said Uncle, "as they seem to be filled with sayings of mine. I shall be interested to see what he has picked out."

"That you are entitled to do, sir, I'm sure," said Woeband. "I've often thought of dipping into them myself when things was a bit quiet but I can't get 'em open."

Uncle, however, could open the small golden books quite easily.

The first one he picked up was a fake book, and hollow inside.

On a piece of gilded parchment was printed: "*Golden Sayings of Uncle. 1.* Hateman is a rotter."

Under the silk was a gold watch inscribed with the words:

Given as a small token to the
owner of Homeward by a grateful
admirer. Ira Smoothy.

"Oh, sir," cried Whitebeard, his eyes gleaming with pleasure at the sight of the gold watch, "what's in the next?"

The next book was hollow too and contained another piece of parchment on which was written: "*Golden Sayings of Uncle. 2. Be upright, pay your rent, avoid brawling and disorder, and you will find me a friend and protector at all times.*"

Uncle read this out to his followers and added:

"It's good for you to have an opportunity to refresh your memories with this particular saying."

"What's under the parchment?" gasped Whitebeard.

"Keep back, Whitebeard," said Uncle.

Under the parchment was a flat golden sardine dish.

"Very nice tokens, very nice indeed," said Uncle. "One goes slogging on in this place with hardly a word of praise, and then, unexpectedly, one finds one has not toiled in vain."

The third golden book contained nothing but a sealed letter.

On the envelope was written: "*Important. To be opened by the Owner of Homeward Castle in private.*"

Uncle pocketed this letter and looked round.

"I shall take this letter home, order refreshments, and then read the letter alone as Mr Ira Smoothy wishes."

"Oh, sir," cried Whitebeard, "can't you just look inside? There might be money!"

"Whitebeard," said Uncle, gravely, "you will have to conquer this money craving. If I had any passing thought of opening that letter before, your remarks have made me absolutely firm against such a step. And now, I think, as we have seen as many wonders as we can take in, we should be going home."

"Oh sir, you must just see one more thing!" cried Woeband. "It's in the sitting-room."

"I think it's about time we had some refreshments," said Uncle. "Where's the One-Armed?"

"Could we have them in the sitting-room, please, sir?" said Woeband. "Then I can tell you about the magic sofa."

While they were eating Woeband explained that the very comfortable-looking sofa which stood just in front of the fireplace had been one that Mr Smoothy used specially for getting rid of visitors who bored him.

"Ah," said Uncle, who, as you know, gets bored very easily, "I should like to see this demonstrated."

"D'you know Colonel Lungy, sir?" asked Woeband. "He lives in a bungalow on the road to Gaby's Marsh."

"I've heard of him, sir," said Goodman. "He was advertising for a manservant in the *Badfort News*."

"Indeed," said Uncle, "he deserves what he gets if he advertises in that rag."

"Colonel Lungy was telling Mr Smoothy a long tale about a boar hunt, and Mr Smoothy invited him to lie down on that sofa – and — "

Woeband began to laugh.

"What happened?" asked Uncle, impatiently.

"You lie down and try it!" cried Woeband.

"No," said Uncle, and turned to Whitebeard. "You do it, Whitebeard, and I'll give you a shilling."

Whitebeard will do nearly anything for money, so he lay down on the sofa and pocketed the shilling.

"Now try to get up," said Woeband.

Whitebeard's happy expression changed to one of horror.

"I can't get up!" he gasped. "I'm held in a sort of vice, sir!"

Woeband went on laughing and then managed to stop enough to say:

"You're a deep 'un, old White Whiskers, but you're caught this time! Give me that shilling and I'll show you how to get up!"

Whitebeard had a fearful mental struggle, but Uncle was watching him closely. With trembling fingers he took the shilling out of his pocket and handed it to Woeband.

"Now," said Woeband, "just say, 'I want to stay here for ever.'"

"I want to stay here for ever," said Whitebeard in rather a frightened voice.

As soon as he had said this he found he could get up quite easily.

Uncle gave him another shilling for behaving so well.

"Mr Smoothy just left Colonel Lungy lying there and went out fishing," said Woeband, gasping and spluttering with laughter.

"Woeband, I cannot see anything amusing in this particular trick," said Uncle, "and as you have taken that shilling from Mr Whitebeard, I will give you half-a-crown instead of the five shillings I was going to give you for showing us round Crack House. Practical jokes can go too far, you know."

"I'm sorry, sir," said Woeband. "With Mr Smoothy being away so much, I misses seeing the tricks in this house tried out, you see. And I don't want nothing from you, sir, not this time. I wanted to make good for what I called you."

"Very well," said Uncle. "It may be as well this time."

There was a light tap on the front door and Woeband went to open it. A. B. Fox stood on the doorstep.

"Well, who are you?" asked Woeband suspiciously. "Never set eyes on you before."

A. B. Fox gave Woeband one piercing look and sauntered past him into the hall. He went up to Uncle at once.

"Afternoon, Fox," said Uncle, and gave him the usual five shillings. "I hope Mrs Bismuth opened the door promptly?"

"I came the country way," said Fox, "past Gaby's Marsh and Colonel Lungy's bungalow. Longish walk through the fields from Badgertown."

"Now I've got the Homeward route cleared up," said Uncle, "I must have a look at this longer route to make sure there are no obstructions in the way for art students. Those good pictures in the Art Gallery should be seen by more people."

"Oh, there won't be any trouble now, sir," said Woeband, "now the crack is empty."

"*And* the syringe has been put away for good," said Uncle.

Woeband looked sad, but quickly handed the Old Monkey the complete version (twenty-nine verses and chorus) of the poem of penitence he had in the pocket of his overall.

"Syringe?" said Fox. "Have you one about?"

"What d'you want it for?" asked Woeband suspiciously.

"Inhabitant of crack is back," said Fox.

Woeband began to dance about in fury, and point at Fox.

"Who's *he* to come in telling us rubbish like that?" he yelled.

"Woeband," said Uncle sternly, "don't forget what happened yesterday. This is Mr Fox, the detective, who has kindly agreed to help us."

"But all our troubles is over here!" snarled Woeband. "We're nice and quiet now!"

"Oblige me by fetching the garden syringe," said Uncle, "and try and show some gratitude, Woeband."

Woeband went off muttering.

Fox held out a packet to Uncle. "Thought we might use some of this," he said, "while we try and find out *why* the creature comes back."

Uncle read what was printed on the label.

Gleamhound's Den Comfort For Pets

Animals sometimes become choosey and tire of their comfortable kennels and cages, and try to escape. Sprinkle the kennel or cage with this powder, and the animal will at once settle down. *Testimonial*: "I had a runaway goat, but now that I've sprinkled its pen with Gleamhound's Den Comfort I can't get it to go out at all."

"There, you see!" said Woeband, who had arrived back with the syringe. "Nice idea that is! Make the horror all comfortable so we're stuck with it! Ve-ry nice, I call that!"

"Woeband," said Uncle, "you have led a quiet life, I know, but you must have heard that all Gleamhound's preparations work backwards. Mr Fox intends to drive the creature away, not keep it here."

Fox dipped the nozzle of the syringe into the packet, and drew the plunger slowly back, then went out of the front door, and walked very quietly along the grass which came right up to the walls of Crack House. As soon as he got to the crack he pointed the syringe up into the hanging ivy and pushed the plunger sharply in.

Then he made a quick loping run back to the front door where the others had all crowded to look out.

"Be ready to get out of the way," he said warningly.

For a moment there was dead silence, while they all craned their necks to see towards the crack.

Then came a series of terrifying sounds. High-pitched squeaks, growls and screams came from the crack. It sounded as if there might be a dozen animals fighting in the darkness there.

Then the curtain of ivy shook and something seemed to be slithering down the crack. A cloud of dust arose, and a shower of rubble fell.

And as they watched, half-fascinated, half-frightened, a most deplorable creature appeared.

"What is it? A bat? A bird?" asked Uncle.

"Bit of both," said Fox.

True, it seemed like an enormous bat, for it had huge black

webbed wings, but unlike a bat it had a sharp beak, and instead of claws folded fists as big as those of a man. Most startling of all, it had lilac-coloured eyes, as big as door-knobs.

"Look out!" snapped Fox, "It's seen us!"

They all shuffled back and he slammed the door.

Just in time.

Almost at once the door was attacked by the furious screaming monster with a beak that battered at the stout oak like a crowbar. Its voice was as sharp and high as a logging-saw.

"Spoil my good den, would you? Spoil my den!" it yelled.

It was terrifying, but the door held.

"Gleamhound's Den Comfort has worked!" said Fox.

"You turkey-snatching fox-brushers, you two-tons-of-sin elephant – you listen to me!"

"Vile language," said Uncle.

"I'd stay here and punish the lot of you skulking in there, I'd pound the whole lot of you to pieces, but the poison, the horrid poison! It's in my mouth! I can't breathe! This poison! This vile poison! I'll come back and peck the lot of you into pieces – little pieces!"

There was another hideous scream, the attack on the door ceased and then came the whirring sounds of great wings rising, rising and going further and further away.

"He's making for Badfort," said Fox, opening the door a little. "Must be a friend of Hateman's!"

They all looked at each other gravely.

NINE

Colonel Lungy

"I FEEL I should like to shake off the foul smell of this creature and go for a short stroll," said Uncle, a few minutes later. "I propose to walk to Colonel Lungy's bungalow. He may have some new facts to tell me about Mr Smoothy."

"He'll wear you out in the telling, if you ask me!" said Woeband.

"I am not asking you, Woeband," said Uncle. "I may say that I feel a certain sympathy with Colonel Lungy. I do not regard it as good manners to fasten a guest, however boring, on to a sofa and go out fishing."

Uncle told Will Shudder, the One-Armed Badger and White-beard to return home by the shorter route, and then ask Clout-man and Gubbins, as soon as they had finished mowing the big lawn, to bring the traction engine to Colonel Lungy's house.

"Where's Fox?" asked Uncle. "He seems to have vanished. I wanted to thank him for his smart work."

Goodman didn't say anything, but he thought he had seen Fox stroll off towards the duck pond. He guessed that A. B. Fox felt the same way about ducks as he himself felt about fish.

Uncle and the Old Monkey and Goodman soon walked out of the shadow of the towers of Homeward into pleasant green fields. The road to Gaby's Marsh meandered quietly through them, and there was little traffic.

"Ah, this does me good!" said Uncle, taking in deep breaths of fresh air.

Soon on the flat land ahead of them they saw a wide and spreading-out sort of tree which seemed to be having a bit of a struggle to live.

"That's a banyan tree," cried the Old Monkey, "from India! They're lovely to climb and swing about in, sir!"

"Ah, Lungy's place, no doubt," said Uncle.

"Can I go and look at it, sir?" asked the Old Monkey. There are not many trees near Homeward and he does miss them.

"You do that," said Uncle. "Goodman and I will ring the bell and announce ourselves."

The Old Monkey scampered ahead, and Uncle and Goodman looked with interest at the small neat bungalow with a veranda running round it. There seemed to be a number of cows and calves grazing in the fields close by.

"Bit of a farmer, eh?" said Uncle.

There was no bell, but a large brass gong by the front door, and this they sounded.

The Colonel himself opened the door. He was tall and somewhat dried-up looking, and wore a clean khaki shirt and very well-pressed khaki trousers.

"Ah, come in, come in!" he said. "The master of the castle of Homeward and attendant! Delightful. Delightful. I know you all

83

by sight, but have never had the pleasure of meeting you, sir. I must apologize for opening the door myself but my man is busy at the back. Well, how pleasant this is! As you can see, I have a distant but good view of your vast palace, sir. As a matter of fact it reminds me very much of the palace of the Rajah of Duk Duk Province. It was one of the wonders of the world! We used to take troops there to see it from Banderush, Osnobagger, Chellsbojerry and another place – the name escapes me for the moment. Let me see, it was Nocharchander. No, I haven't got it quite right. It began with N, that I do remember. Wait, wait, I'll get it!"

As he talked he led them to a sitting-room simply crammed with brass-topped tables, bowls and sets of temple bells on racks.

"Don't trouble, Colonel," said Uncle, hastily. "I have come to ask you about a Mr Ira Smoothy."

"Ah, Smoothy," said Colonel Lungy, hesitatingly. "Yes, interesting fellow. A self-made man, I should judge, but none the worse for that, of course. Used to see a lot of him at one time, but there was one unfortunate incident. He's a bit of a practical joker, you know, and I'm not as young as I was. Can't take it as I used to. Still, never mind. He travels a lot, and I'm occupied with my pedigree stock. I don't see much of him, but he's a clever man, and — "

"Do you know why he left Crack House?" asked Uncle, managing to get a word in at last.

"Said the place was haunted," said Colonel Lungy, "by a *smell* as much as anything else! I don't mind ghosts myself. There was one rest-house in the jungle near Chellapoona that was so haunted your hair will stand on end as I tell you. It was in the middle of the monsoon period and I, with a small party — "

"Some other time, Colonel," said Uncle. "It is getting somewhat late in the day, and I have pressing duties to attend to. But I'm glad to have met you, and hope all goes well with you."

"Extremely well," said Colonel Lungy, "particularly today, for after many efforts I have managed to get a new manservant as a result of an advert. in the *Badfort News*. No result from other papers. My other servants never stayed, and yet I used to entertain them night after night with thrilling accounts of life in the East. I can't understand it."

"Tell me, what is your new man like?" asked Uncle.

"Bit of a rough cove. Wears a sack suit, and his hair isn't at all well cut, and I must look out another pair of boots for him, but he'll be all right. Come and see him at work in the back room. He's got a pile of ashes out of the grate. Nobody else has cleaned up so well, and he's busy now polishing my presentation mugs and salvers."

He led them eagerly to the next room where a shocking, but not altogether unexpected, sight met Uncle's gaze.

Beaver Hateman was stooping over a large sack, and as the door opened was trying to cram a golden goblet into the mouth of it.

"As I thought!" said Uncle in a voice of thunder.

"Now what's the matter with you – you big stiff!" shouted Beaver Hateman. "Haven't you ever seen a butler collecting silver for cleaning before?"

"This man," said Uncle to Colonel Lungy, "is about to rob you of your most valuable possessions!"

"Oh, surely not!" said Colonel Lungy.

"I know him," said Uncle. "I know him well!"

"And I know *him*!" yelled Beaver Hateman, pointing at Uncle. "He's the biggest liar in the world! He's a nice one to talk about stealing! He stole a bike once from a poor student."

This story about the day when Uncle borrowed a bike at the University to get to an examination in time is always being brought up by the Hateman gang. It's wearisome, and maddening.

Uncle was trying to keep his temper, and at that moment the Old Monkey came rushing up to the open french window.

"Oh sir," he cried, "Jellytussle is outside trying to get two of the Colonel's valuable calves into the Wooden-Legged Donkey's cart!"

"What!" cried Lungy. "My prize calves! Never!"

"Jellytussle has got the calves out of the pen, and he's told them to get into the cart and wait there for Hateman and the bag of silver," gasped the Old Monkey.

"Who are these blackguards?" shouted Lungy. "Stop them! Stop them!"

He dashed outside, after seizing a boar-lance from his hat-stand, followed by Goodman and the Old Monkey.

What a sight met their eyes! The traction engine from Homeward, manned by Cloutman and Gubbins, had just arrived, and without waiting to be told what it was all about Uncle's two strong men had dashed into the fight. Gubbins had grasped Jellytussle in his fearful grip, while Cloutman aimed a heavy blow at the don-

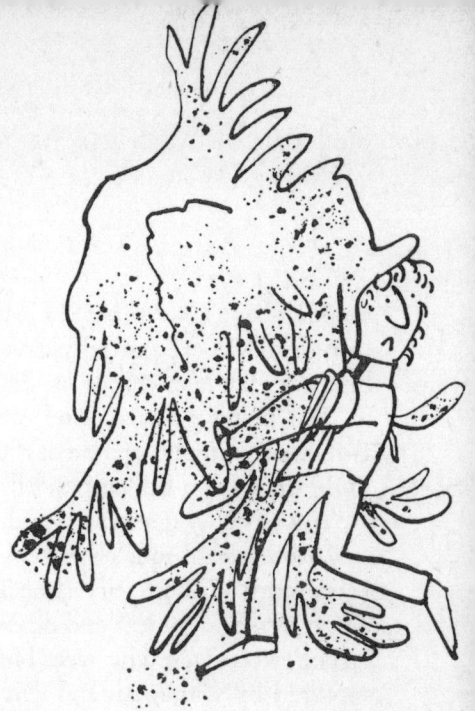

key who lashed out with his wooden leg. The cart was upset and the calves were set free. Gubbins knew, from experience, how difficult it was to fight with Jellytussle. No good just hitting at his layers of quivering jelly. He grasped him and his arms sank deep into the odious jelly, but at last he got a firm grip on the solid body underneath.

Meanwhile Uncle and Beaver Hateman were left face to face.

"Your interfering old gas-bag!" yelled Beaver. "Everything was going fine till you turned up! Ever seen a grate cleaned out like this? Hadn't been touched for weeks!"

And he picked up the bucket of ashes and threw the contents over Uncle. Half-blinded as he was, Uncle saw Hateman make a leap for the french window, and, charging through the brass-topped tables, scattering them right and left, he caught Beaver Hateman with a kick just as he was dashing through into the open air.

It was really one of his very best kicks.

Hateman rose high, high, into the air, right above the banyan tree, out of which flew a number of outraged parrots. The kick couldn't have taken place at a better moment, for just as Gubbins's iron grip was causing Jellytussle to collapse, from far up in the blue sky Hateman was descending with the force of a meteorite.

"Hateman's going to land on Jellytussle! He is! He is!" cried Goodman, running up one of the veranda posts in his excitement. "Oh, sir, what a brilliant kick!"

"It was richly deserved," said Uncle. "I need say no more!"

With a horrid squelch Hateman did land smack on Jellytussle. More strips of bluish jelly came floating up, and Jellytussle uttered a cry, tremblingly soft and odiously quivering.

The two calves, who were blundering about bewildered, were captured by Cloutman and driven into their pen. They seemed glad to be back, and ready to lick Colonel Lungy's hand as he anxiously examined them for damage.

"Splendid!" said Uncle to Cloutman and Gubbins. "You couldn't have arrived at a more useful time."

Injured and bruised as they were, Jellytussle and Hateman managed to crawl into the cart.

"You'll suffer for this!" yelled Hateman, shaking his fist at Uncle. "You'll suffer! A full account in the *Badfort News* is only the beginning!"

Then the Wooden-Legged Donkey recovered, and they vanished into the distance yelling and hooting.

Lungy was quite overpowered.

"I owe you and your splendid retinue a deep debt of gratitude," he said to Uncle. "Your swift action reminds me of a time when I was able to aid a visiting prince in the Province of Shotconjuberry, or was it Shutvanjuberry? No matter, I'll think the names out afterwards. Meanwhile you must be cleaned of ash, sir, and I must provide what refreshments I can."

Uncle had shaken off a lot of the ashes in his swift rush after Hateman, and luckily the Old Monkey had with him a tin of

Gleamhound's Sticky Dust. The instructions were: "Simply dust the area evenly. The person dusted will immediately be covered with a sticky powder that will disable him for hours."

"This will soon clean you up, sir," said the Old Monkey.

As you know Gleamhound's remedies work backwards, so after one application Uncle's clothes were perfectly clean, and the Old Monkey went to help Goodman brush up the ashes in the back room.

Lungy had by now made a nice little feast ready in the front room and summoned them by striking a descending scale of notes on his brass temple bells.

There were Scander Biscuits from Hum-Hum Province, Tortoise Pies (preserved) from Mallaby Ranch, Global Globules from a little village in America, and a tin of Python Whiffets. Uncle avoided the Python Whiffets, though Colonel Lungy told him they had been much enjoyed by the High Commissioner of Slingum Territory.

While they ate, Uncle had been thinking out a way of providing Colonel Lungy with a new helper. He liked the Colonel very much in spite of his fearfully boring stories.

"I know an old man called Whitebeard," he said at last, "who is quite honest but extremely fond of money. I'm sure if you give him a modest sum to sit with you in the evenings and listen to your stories he will be very pleased to come. He listens to my brother Rudolph, the traveller and big-game hunter, for hours, as long as he gets a penny or two at the end. Shall I ask him?"

"Please do," said Colonel Lungy. "He sounds just the man for me."

"And now we must go," said Uncle as they walked out on to the veranda. "I can see the sun is beginning to set beyond the towers of Homeward."

But he didn't manage to get away before Lungy had taken

down from a shelf a small gold-lined mug with an elephant on the handle and given it to uncle as a token. He also added to this gift a tin of Python Whiffets.

As they went down the path, Colonel Lungy was telling them:

"The names on the mug will interest you. Challender Duk is one, Vidsnaffle Boonbat another — "

And as the traction engine began to move he shouted:

"I've remembered one or two more of the names – Soonswan, Sinnablit and Zeelongfingo — "

There seemed to be others, but they were lost as the traction engine chugged towards Homeward.

That evening, while Uncle was talking over with the Old Monkey and Goodman the strange events of the day, a copy of the *Badfort News* was thrust through the letter-box.

"Read it out," said Uncle to Goodman, "and then put it on the fire as usual."

Goodman read:

Badfort News. Special Edition.

"A new and horrible outrage is reported. Dear good Uncle has outdone himself in a deed so abominable that it's a wonder this paper doesn't shrivel up as the story is put down.

"Mr Beaver Hateman had accepted a post as gentleman's gentleman with Colonel Lungy, of Gaby's Marsh, and was carrying out his silver-cleaning duties when in burst Fatty Fury who vilely accused him of stealing a goblet.

"This is the fat dictator of Homeward, who lies so much that he gets toothache if he tells the truth.

"Rise citizens, smash his mouldy castle and let us breathe again!"

"Enough!" said Uncle. "Burn the rag and bring me a drink of Koolvat!"

TEN

A Call and an Interview

THE *Badfort News* had hardly stopped burning in the grate before the telephone rang. The Old Monkey came back from answering it much excited.

"It's from Mr Smoothy, sir. He says he's in a call box and has no change. Will you pay for the call, sir?"

"He ought to have change," said Uncle, irritated. "However, I want to get in touch with him, so he'd better reverse the charges. How much is it?"

"He says it's seven-and-ninepence already, sir."

"That's pretty stiff," said Uncle, stalking to the telephone. "Wherever can he be calling from?"

As soon as Uncle picked up the receiver a harsh voice said:

"Is that the owner of the castle of Homeward – the benefactor of the whole region?"

"It is," said Uncle. "But cut it short or there'll be another seven-and-ninepence to pay."

"Sorry, but I had nothing but a ten-pound note in my pocket. I'm calling from Jubber's Pull-Up on the other side of Badfort. I'm on my way back to Crack House. You got my letter?"

"I brought it home from Crack House," said Uncle, "but how d'you know? I've only had it a few hours."

"My good sir," said Smoothy, "as I was travelling towards Gaby's Marsh I saw a horrible bat-like creature flying towards Badfort from the Crack House region of Homeward. That's it, I thought. That's the creature that made my life a misery. Nobody but the owner of Homeward could be powerful enough to get rid of it. So I knew you'd been to my house. Have you read the letter yet?"

"No," said Uncle. "I was going to make arrangements to do so privately, as you asked."

"I'd like you to burn it. Will you oblige me?"

"Certainly," said Uncle.

"I know your servants are faithful, but you are surrounded by enemies, and I much regret having written the letter at all in case it gets into the wrong hands. It contains a copy of an old manuscript I have in my possession, and I thought if I never returned from my travels you would be the person to entrust with the information contained in it."

"I am honoured," said Uncle. "The letter is perfectly safe with me."

"All the same, will you burn it at once? I'm taking no chances."

"All right," said Uncle.

"I'll hold on while you do it."

The letter was soon burnt, and Uncle went back to the telephone.

"Is that you, Smoothy?"

"Yes, but they want eight-and-ninepence for an extended call. Did you break up the ashes?"

"Yes, I did," shouted Uncle, with a roar that nearly shattered the telephone. "Now get to the point or I'll ring off!"

Smoothy gave a loud laugh.

"Right you are," he said. "I kinda like your way of doing business. You're the man for me. I'm coming to see you."

"Tonight?"

"Yes, the sooner the better. No secret passages leading from your living-room?"

"I won't swear to that," said Uncle. "Nearly all my rooms have secret passages."

"That's bad, but we'll manage. I'll be with you in half-an-hour. And I'd like to be put up for the night, if you don't mind. It's a bit late for pushing on to Crack House. I can doss down on the floor, and I won't need feeding. I always carry with me a bag of Double Grass Fizz Cakes and they'll provide me with ample nourishment."

"The charge is now nine-and-ninepence," said the operator.

"Oh, shut up!" said Uncle.

"Oh, is that you, sir?" said a meek voice. "There's a special charge for you, sir. Sixpence for as long as you like."

"I should think so!" said Uncle.

"I'm starting off now on my motor-bike," said Smoothy. Then he rang off.

As the arrival of Smoothy was rather an important event, Uncle put on his second-best purple dressing-gown for the occasion.

Soon they heard a motor-bicycle outside, and then, as the engine stopped, a most melodious horn was sounded. Listening to it was like hearing the opening of some great piece of music. They were all surprised at the very delicious sounds.

Most of Uncle's followers rushed to the door to look out, but Uncle stayed where he was by the fire as he thought it was more dignified.

"Oh, sir," cried Goodman, rushing back from the door. "Mr Smoothy has got the biggest motor-bike I've seen. It's nearly as big as a car and covered with gadgets!"

Smoothy was a short, immensely broad man with thick hair brushed aggressively up, horn-rimmed glasses, and a couple of pistols in his belt. He stamped up the stairs, chewing on his nails.

Uncle was a little surprised at his somewhat savage appearance, but pleased because he immediately threw off his pistol belt. He also put a ten-pound note on the table.

"Sorry about the guns," he said, "but I've been through some pretty wild country. They're really just stinging pistols, but nobody knows that. The money is for telephone and lodging for the night. I don't invite myself without paying."

"I don't accept payment from guests, Mr Smoothy," said Uncle.

"Well, I guess you don't need to by the look of this place," said Smoothy, glancing round. "I'm not much of a judge of art but that picture of you opening those fountains is smashing. Give the money to somebody who needs it, then, but not to that old cove with the white whiskers, if you don't mind my saying so. He's a miser, if I've got any eyes at all."

Whitebeard put on his best poverty-stricken look as Uncle picked up the note.

"Thank you, I will see somebody deserving gets this," said Uncle, "and now we will show you to your room, and you must have a meal."

"I've got plenty of Double Grass Fizz Cakes with me, and I should like a kip in front of that splendid fire. Your handsome cat will keep the rats off!"

Goodman gave a pleased purr.

"And now," said Uncle, who liked Smoothy in spite of his rough manner, "it's getting late, and we've had a long day. If you are determined to talk before we turn in let's start at once."

Uncle led the way to a small private room that he very seldom uses. It was made of one block of steel, and was, as far as Uncle could judge, absolutely free from secret passages. There were just two chairs set in the middle of the floor.

"Now," said Uncle, as he locked the door. "This place is sound-proof. I had it tested by having twenty brass bands playing around it. I couldn't hear a thing."

This seemed to impress Smoothy more than anything else Uncle had said.

He looked at Uncle solemnly. "I say, you do do things in style!" he said.

"Thank you. Now what do you wish to speak to me about?" asked Uncle.

Smoothy leaned forward until his face was nearly inside Uncle's gigantic ear.

"I have reason to believe there is buried treasure of immense value near Crack House."

"Deeply interesting," said Uncle. "Go on."

Smoothy drew from an inner pocket a small yellow roll tied up with very old and dirty tape. When he got it unfolded – and doing that made a loud cracking noise – Uncle saw a lot of strange dark writing on it. Letters like toppling steeples and towers tottered after each other across the stiff yellow parchment. It seemed impossible to read it.

"This was handed down to me with the deeds of Crack House!" muttered Smoothy. "And it is a copy of this that was in the letter I asked you to burn."

"Speak up," said Uncle, "nobody can hear! Can you read this thing?"

"I got an expert on old manuscripts to read it. It's a sort of poem."

"It's not long, so let's hear it," said Uncle.

Smoothy drew his chair even closer and read:

> "Syt ye no more by ye fyre in ye halle
> > like ye hogge
> But search ye aboute with ye long smalle snout
> > for ye dlog
> Not to ye sky shall ye turne uppe ye eye
> > but like dogge
> Snuffle around with ye nose to ye ground
> > for ye dlog."

"Ah," said Uncle, "interesting little poem."

"Dlog is gold, of course," said Smoothy.

"I see," said Uncle, who did now that he'd been told.

"Digging must have been going on for years and years," said Smoothy. "Chap I bought the place from said the crack was made by his grandfather. He tried a pinch of dynamite to hurry things up. Before that the house was called Prosperity Lodge."

"Tried digging yourself?" asked Uncle.

"Of course," said Smoothy, "and by now I'd have found something if I had been able to live in peace there. That disgusting bird-bat came to live in the crack soon after I got there. It's no good, that creature and I can't live side by side. I've tried everything to get rid of him. Fumigation. Chucked in a lot of thousand-year oil. Nothing shifted him. In the end it was either him or me, so I decided to clear off for a bit. I don't like the smell of bat, and it wasn't *just* that. It was the screaming and squeaking at night. You couldn't get any sleep."

"I gathered things were bad from the Snowjuices," said Uncle. "I felt something had to be done to clear the monster out finally and solve the mystery. I have employed a detective to advise me."

"Not A. B. Fox?" cried Smoothy.

"Yes."

Smoothy slapped Uncle on the knee so hard that he couldn't help wincing.

"We'll get somewhere with that chap Fox on it," he said.

"Fox gave it as his opinion that the creature wouldn't stay away for long."

"He's right," said Smoothy. "If you ask me, he's after the treasure as well. I don't really need any treasure myself, and I guess you don't, but until it is found there'll be no peace at Crack House. So we'd better find it. We'll share out whatever there is and do a bit of good with it. What d'you say?"

"Agreed," said Uncle.

"And meanwhile not a word!" whispered Smoothy.

"Not a word!" said Uncle.

"That's settled, then. Tomorrow I'll go back to Crack House and try to get started. How's Woeband been behaving? Not writing any more poems, I hope."

"Only one," said Uncle. "Rather good, but too long."

"They're always too long," said Smoothy.

"He showed us round Crack House this afternoon and kept right off poetry. He's a great admirer of your gadgets. I must say you have some remarkable things!"

"I've put in a lot of improvements," said Smoothy, "and will do more if I can have a bit of peace. I plan to keep Woeband for the rough work. I'm bringing a butler with me this time. A lion called Leominster. He's pretty impressive. You should see him carry in a trencher of dressed crabs. Very splendid and grand."

"I don't go in for butlers much myself, but I'll be interested to meet him," said Uncle. "And now let's go and have supper with the others. I've had about enough of this stuffy little den."

So they left the sound-proof room and had a merry supper. Smoothy handed round some Double Grass Fizz Cakes which were very popular.

ELEVEN

A Visitor from Badfort

SMOOTHY was offered a room with a beautiful bed that night, but he had taken a fancy to sleeping in front of the great fire in the hall. It was cheerful and comfortable, all bright and glittering with ornaments and pictures, and with plenty of cushions and rugs. Goodman the cat just dozed and kept an eye open for rats.

Smoothy was snoring before Uncle got to the top of the stairs. He was rather better-looking asleep than awake, Uncle thought.

Soon after midnight Smoothy woke. He has very keen hearing and he felt sure somebody was at the door. He realized he had been right when Goodman came padding softly up to him and whispered:

"There's somebody outside, Mr Smoothy. Somebody shuffling about and crackling paper."

"But it's after midnight," said Smoothy, glancing at his wrist-watch, which was about the size of a saucer and lit up when anyone looked at it. "Nice time to deliver papers."

"It'll be from Badfort," whispered Goodman. "*They* stay awake most of the night."

"Keep your eye on that letter-box," hissed Smoothy.

They stayed very still by the fire. As they watched, a shabby-looking newspaper fell through the letter-box. The slit was then held open by a large dirty hand. A pair of glittering eyes under a fringe of hair came into view. The hall was dark except for firelight, but this shone into them and made them seem red.

"Hateman!" whispered Goodman.

"The Big Boss of Badfort?"

Goodman nodded.

Smoothy got to his feet, picking up the can of Koolvat the Old Monkey had left for him to drink during the night.

"Bit early with the papers, boy, aren't you?" he said in his rasping voice.

"I'm no paper boy!" yelled Hateman. "And who are you, you great greasy lounge-lizard, snoozing by the fire, stuffed with food, pistols on the table, hobnobbing with that cheeky cat? Just the sort of friend the Dictator *would* have!"

Smoothy lifted the can of Koolvat and flung it through the letter-box with such skill that it splashed with stinging force right into Hateman's face.

There was a furious yell, the face disappeared, and the box snapped shut.

Smoothy and Goodman looked at each other and smiled as Hateman hissed:

"You'll suffer for flinging that stinking Koolvat! Suffer for months and years!"

Gradually the sounds of coughing and spluttering grew fainter.

"He's gone," said Goodman. "That was a smart piece of work, Mr Smoothy."

"Let's have a look at that paper," said Smoothy.

"It's the *Badfort News*," said Goodman. "It's sure to be a horrible attack of some sort. It will keep you awake all night if you read it."

"Oh no, it won't," said Smoothy.

Smoothy put on his glasses and with Goodman looking over his shoulder read:

BACK TO BARBARISM

We feel it is our duty to tell our readers that the Dictator, under whose iron hoof we struggle to live, has found a new method of injury, more foul, more atrocious than any he had tried before.

He has used POISON GAS!

Poison gas which has been given up by all civilized beings. Except by the Dictator. Poison gas was used against a most respectable citizen called Batty, who because he was too poor to have a home lived a most peaceful and harmless life in a crack in the wall of an old empty house.

It is not enough for the Dictator to have more rooms than he can possibly use. He has to turn out a poor inoffensive citizen from his modest shelter with a blast of poison. Weak and ill, Batty flew to Badfort to ask for shelter from Mr Hateman who willingly gave it. How long must we tolerate this? Rise in thousands against the smiling poisoner.

"Well, well," said Smoothy, "quite a piece. Batty is the name of that pest, is it? And what was this poison, if any?"

"Just Gleamhound's Den Comfort For Pets," said Goodman. "It works backwards, you know."

"No, I did not," said Smoothy, "but I'm pretty interested to hear this. Pretty interested. And now let's get some sleep and forget the wretched Batty for a bit."

Although Goodman stayed awake for some time longer, keeping a keen look out, Smoothy went to sleep at once and didn't wake till breakfast was on the table. This time he was content to have a normal meal with the others, merely adding a couple of thin flat cakes called Seaweed Slashers out of his pocket to eat with his ham.

"Heffo's late with the letters this morning," said Uncle.

"But this came during the night," said Smoothy, "and I took the liberty of reading it."

"That vile rag!" said Uncle, and took a strengthening draught of cocoa before putting on his glasses.

When he had read it he and Smoothy looked at each other gravely.

"So this proves that Batty is a spy for the Hateman gang," said Uncle. "I need say no more."

Smoothy took the biggest automatic lighter Uncle had ever seen from his pocket. It was shaped like a banana, and he just pinched the top and a great flame sprang out. Then he burnt the shameful rag.

"I'm not a squeamish man," he said, "but that loathsome screed made me feel downright ill."

His speech was interrupted by the Old Monkey who came rushing in.

"The ambulance from Badgertown Hospital is at the door, sir."

"Ambulance?" said Uncle. "Who for? Nobody is ill here!"

"Oh, no, sir," said the Old Monkey. "It's Mr Linseed on his way to hospital!"

There was a shuffling sound outside the door, and Linseed appeared supported by two strong young bears in the uniform of ambulance attendants.

He seemed almost too weak to walk, and collapsed on to a large sofa and burst into tears.

"Now, Linseed, drink this," said Uncle, and handed him a jug of Koolvat. At last he managed to speak.

"Oh, sir," he said, "things went on getting worse and worse after I saw you, and at last I plucked up courage and took your advice and told Hateman that I was leaving Badfort, but I had the deeds and Badfort was still mine. I said steps would be taken to turn him out. He started to laugh, and his laugh was so loud it split my last unbroken tumblers and they all fell from a shelf. And then he asked me to show him the deeds."

"You did, of course?" said Uncle.

"Yes, and do you know what I saw, sir – ?"

Linseed seemed unable to go on. Smoothy came forward with a Double Grass Fizz Cake, and after a few seconds of quiet munching he gathered up a little strength.

"The sheets of parchment making up the deeds were *blank*, sir. Quite *blank*. They were drawn up in wizard ink, Hateman said. The writing looks all right for a day or so and then vanishes. So I have nothing left to show lawyers and prove that Badfort is mine!"

"This is atrocious work!" said Uncle.

"Then the whole gang was on me, kicking, biting, pushing. At last they flung me out of the front door on to a pile of ashes, and there I stayed till a young passing badger took a message to the hospital. When I come out I think I'll stay with Dearman for a while as I hear he has a couple of rooms to let over his shop. I'd ask you to put me up but I can't stand the sight of Badfort."

"I agree," said Uncle. "If you are to recover your health you need to get away. What does Dearman charge?"

"Sixpence a week to begin with, but next week it's doubled,

and the next week doubled again. I thought I'd stay a week or two at the low price."

"I should advise you to have a straight talk with Dearman," said Uncle, "and make him a firm straight offer for a reasonable rent. Later we must discuss a fresh start in business for you. Those police snacks sounded a good line to me."

"Oh, they were! If only I'd stuck to them I'd still be a prosperous man!" wailed Linseed.

"And don't stay too long at Dearman's!" said Whitebeard, who had been doing a long sum on an old envelope. "D'you realize if you stay three months with him you'll be paying over £100 a week?"

"Starting at sixpence?"

Uncle could hardly believe this, but Smoothy took the envelope and examined the figures. They went like this:

> 1st week 6d.
> 2nd week 1s.

And so on, down to:

> 13th week £102 8s. 0d.

"Old Shavepenny is right," he said. "You'd better look out."

After Linseed had been helped into the ambulance with a bunch of bananas to aid his recovery, Smoothy went out to his motor-bike, strapping on his pistol belt.

"Thanks for your hospitality," he said to Uncle. "I'll let you know at once if anything happens at Crack House. I now know what I'm up against, and I feel a lot better knowing I have your support and that of A. B. Fox."

With a melodious burst of sound from his huge horn he rode away.

TWELVE

Uncle's Pantry

As nothing could be done about searching for the buried treasure till Smoothy had settled in at Crack House, Uncle thought he would have a quiet day and get on with dictating the story of his life to Will Shudder, after he had read the morning paper.

He was just turning the pages over and thinking how pleasant it was to have no arrangements on hand, when a very loud buzzer sounded. That's my pantry buzzer, thought Uncle, and means somebody has closed the door. Why?

Usually Uncle and his followers don't bother to shut the door during the day because the buzzer makes an almost unbearable noise when it is either opened or shut. This device is very useful against thieves, of course.

Uncle was just about to send for the Old Monkey when A. B. Fox came in.

"Here's your five bob, Fox," said Uncle. "Who closed the pantry door?"

"You've got trouble in your pantry," said A. B. Fox.

"Trouble? In my pantry?" Uncle was outraged.

He threw down his paper and hurried to the pantry with Fox.

Uncle is very proud of his pantry. Just inside the door is the Butter Walk, where the walls are lined with thousands of packets of butter. By the door is the big table where the Old Monkey keeps one slab of butter, about a hundredweight, for daily use. It lasts most of the day and is very handy.

Next comes the Lard Entry. Here all the walls are built of kegs and boxes of lard. You might think it would look a bit dull being all lard, but it doesn't. A lot of the lard is packed in shining containers and some of the kegs are painted green and pink, so it looks very bright.

In the pantry itself the ceiling is pink and has little pink lights in it. Hundreds of tins are stacked on the shelves, and with the lights on it looks like a palace.

Right in the middle is a gigantic table. There is a meat slicer at one end, and a weighing machine at the other. This weighing machine is so exact that it can weigh half an ounce of sugar, and yet it can also take the greatest weights.

Uncle often weighs himself on it when he thinks he is getting too fat.

The huge table had recently been cut away to make a space for a refrigerator. This had been given to Uncle by his brother Rudolph, the explorer and big-game hunter. It was a very special and large present, and Rudolph had had great difficulty in getting it past the Badfort crowd and safely to Homeward. He had only been able to do so by disguising himself as a van-man driving a huge van labelled:

POSH PIKELETS FOR POSH PEOPLE

Outside the closed pantry door, when Uncle and Fox got there, stood the Old Monkey looking very worried.

"Oh, sir," he cried, "there's somebody in the refrigerator, groaning and shuffling about!"

"Groaning and shuffling about – in *my* refrigerator!" shouted Uncle. "This is abominable. I keep my choicest foods there! Let's get to the bottom of this at once!"

The door of the pantry just had the word PANTRY printed on it in huge letters. Under the word hangs a large frying pan on a hook. There are no bolts, bars, handles or push-buttons. Unless you know the secret it seems impossible to get in.

What you have to understand is that the word Pantry means PAN TRY. Then it's easy.

While Uncle waited fuming, the Old Monkey simply moved the pan sideways and a hidden catch was released.

At once the door opened and the buzzer sounded. As they

couldn't speak at all while it was sounding they marched quickly through the Butter Walk and Lard Entry to the pantry itself.

As soon as they reached the refrigerator Uncle bent close to it. He could hear a feeble groaning and muttering inside.

"This refrigerator was given to me for the storage of choice gifts!" he said. "I'll have no thieves lurking in it."

He swung the heavy door open.

What a horrible sight met his gaze! There, feebly propped against the pale-blue wall, was the wretched dwarf Hitmouse. At his feet stood a bag full of tins and glass containers. The half-dozen or so skewers he always carries had had their ends dipped into a jug of orange juice and were frozen together. Even his hating book, also damp with orange juice, was frozen to the back of his coat. He looked pretty ill.

"Pull him out and set him by the hot pipes to thaw," Uncle told Fox.

"You rotten lot of butchers!" shivered Hitmouse, between chattering teeth. "Freezing a h-honest r-reporter to d-death. This'll look good in the *Badfort News*!"

"Extraordinary!" said Uncle. "Even when iced-up Hitmouse can spit venom!"

"Oh, sir, he's been eating the tin of Python Whiffets Colonel Lungy gave you!" said the Old Monkey.

"R-r-ank p-p-poison!" chattered Hitmouse, one blue hand reaching for a skewer. "If it hadn't been for those rotten Whiffets I'd have k-k-kept my f-f-oot in the door and not got sh-shut in!"

"You came to steal," said Uncle. "The door of the refrigerator is self-closing and shut you in, as you deserved!"

"Who'd want your poisonous old food! Loin of pork was what I was after!" screamed Hitmouse, who was getting stronger every minute. "I only stepped in there to avoid Fox when he came poking round. I was shadowing him in the course of my newspaper work."

"New name for stealing," said Fox, picking up the bag which had been at Hitmouse's feet. "Bag contains Juba Jelly, Stingo Steak, and Whooshmeat," he said.

Uncle was deeply shocked. Juba Jelly is £1 17s. 6d. for a quarter-pound tin, Stingo Steak, only eaten by Kings of the Stingo Tribe, is £3 a slice. Whooshmeat is hardly obtainable now as the Whoosh deer is extinct, but the market price of the little that is left is £7 per ounce.

"Wish I'd left the Python Whiffets for you to swallow!" said Hitmouse in his usual bitter tones. "They'd have given you a very bad pain like they have me!"

"Keep your horrible wishes to yourself!" said Uncle, but he was secretly pleased. He had always felt doubtful about the

Python Whiffets and had hoped Lungy would never ask how he liked them. Now Hitmouse had cleared the way. He would be able to tell the Colonel that the whiffets had been stolen after they had been put away in what seemed a safe place.

"What's he doing here? What d'you want a detective for?" shouted Hitmouse. "You're up to no good — any of you."

"Let's get rid of him," said Uncle to the Old Monkey. "He's suffered enough in the cold. Just call Cloutman to see he gets over the moat, and doesn't sneak back!"

By the time Hitmouse had got to the front door he was strong enough to throw a skewer at Uncle, but it fell short.

"We're watching you!" he shouted, as Cloutman seized him. "You and your rotten detective. Whatever you're up to we'll find it out, that's certain!"

"Get this revolting food-snatcher out of my sight!" said Uncle.

Goodman came rushing in as the door closed behind Hitmouse. He had been in the library with Will Shudder, licking stamps and putting them on letters ever since breakfast, and had missed the whole pantry episode. He had once been the only person to be suspicious of Hitmouse when he tried to disguise himself as a little girl in order to deceive Uncle, and he was very disappointed not to have been on hand when Fox took Uncle to the pantry.

"I call it pretty mean of you all leaving me out!" he said. "You know Hitmouse is *my* special enemy! I'm always keeping an eye open for Hitmouse! You might have called me! You might have called me!"

"Goodman," said Uncle, "you sometimes forget yourself. Duty comes first, you know."

"But catching Hitmouse *is* duty – " Goodman began.

Fox interrupted him. "I'm taking a stroll to Crack House. What about coming with me, Goodman? We could have a look at the ducks."

Fox winked at Goodman and Uncle saw this.

"Remember, Fox," said Uncle, "that the ducks, noisy and troublesome as they are, happen to be tenants of mine and are therefore under my protection."

Fox looked slightly ashamed of himself as he sauntered off with Goodman.

"Goodman was really very disappointed, sir," said the Old Monkey, "not to see Hitmouse caught."

"I think," said Uncle, "that we'll be able to make up to him a little for his disappointment. I've decided that it's useless to store up these special dainties too long. We might as well have a special feast tonight of some of the things Hitmouse tried to steal."

So they did. The general feeling was that the price of most of them was too high.

They only had a spoonful each of the Whooshmeat. It tasted perhaps a little better than ordinary venison, but barely worth £7 per ounce. On the whole they liked Stingo Steak just as well, and it was a lot cheaper. At the end, as a relish, they had one quarter-pound tin of Juba Jelly between them. The taste of this was really lovely. There was no doubt about it, Juba Jelly was the real winner. The good taste lasted so long, too. They were still feeling warmed and cheered by it when they went to bed.

THIRTEEN

A Rural Ride

DURING the next day or so Uncle was sorry to see that all the Badfort crowd were back in their shabby fortress. Jellytussle was there, of course, and all the Hateman family, Flabskin, Oily Joe, and most ominous of all the vague shadowy figure of Hootman. Hootman is a kind of ghost, but not much liked by real ghosts because he's so spiteful. He always appears when some big plot against Uncle is being thought out. Beaver Hateman seems to depend on his advice.

Fresh trouble could shortly be expected, that was clear.

One morning Uncle had just finished dealing with his letters when the Old Monkey came in to say that three of the Respectable Horses had called. There are four Respectable Horses, Mayhave Crunch and his three sisters Anna, Ann and Annette. They always look extremely neat and tidy in their shining black coats with a patch of white on the necks that looks very like a clergyman's collar. It was the three sisters who had called today.

"Ask them to come in," said Uncle, "and bring in a bucket of Koolvat."

The three sisters sat on one of the flat sofas, their well-brushed hooves shining, and each sipped in turn at the Koolvat.

"We have been planning a little trip round Homeward to Crack House," the eldest of the sisters, Miss Anna, said at last, "and would be so happy if you, sir, and the Old Monkey, and any other of your followers you care to bring, would come with us. We have just received news that an old family friend, Mr Leominster, has taken a post with Mr Smoothy, and we would so like to see him and talk over old times. My sisters and I have recently spent some of our savings on an open carriage, not new, but very roomy, and we can easily pull it. We thought you might like a ride with us."

"It's extremely kind, ladies," said Uncle, "and I am greatly taken with the idea, I must say."

The Old Monkey was actually standing on one foot in suspense, he was so eager to go.

"Mr Smoothy did ring up to ask if you could go to Crack House soon, didn't he, sir?" he said.

"Yes," said Uncle, "and I have various important matters to discuss with him, but I am worried by one point. Is your carriage strong enough? I am not fat, but I am a good weight."

"We have considered this and are sure the carriage will be perfectly safe, aren't we, sisters?"

"Yes, indeed," said Ann and Annette together, "perfectly safe."

"Unfortunately our brother Mayhave Crunch is away at a Conference of Carriage Horses, but he sends his regards and good wishes for a happy excursion."

"I'd like to look in at the Art Gallery as well," said Uncle, "and make sure Waldovenison Smeare has got the Old Masters well housed, and also that the Snowjuices are free from trouble at night. It will be a novelty to ride in a carriage, so thank you very much."

"We have left the carriage outside and can start at once, if that is agreeable," said Miss Anna, "and we have a well-filled hamper in the boot."

"I can see you have thought of everything, ladies," said Uncle, and then heard a small sob behind him. The One-Armed Badger was ready, loaded to the ground with provisions, and overcome with disappointment at the thought that he might be left behind.

"Well, if you agree, the One-Armed can come too," Uncle said to the Respectable Horses. "The Snowjuices will be glad of any provisions we have to spare."

So it was settled. Uncle, the Old Monkey, Goodman and Will Shudder were to go. Cloutman and Gubbins were to stay behind and keep an eye on Badfort as there was so much activity there, and Uncle rang up Captain Walrus, who lives on a lighthouse at

the extreme edge of Lion Tower, to tell him to keep a sharp look-out through his glasses and take the express lift down to Homeward to help Cloutman and Gubbins if necessary.

The carriage was somewhat crowded, but the Old Monkey got up into the driver's seat and that eased things. He didn't drive, of course. The Respectable Horses are never driven. They just place themselves between the shafts and start off.

It was a lovely journey. No cracking of whips or finding of directions, just smooth leisurely travelling.

To begin with, they rode by the shining waters of the moat. The road here was bordered by foxgloves and lilies, as if for a royal procession. The vast walls of Homeward were on one side, but the sun shone on them and they cast no shadows. As he rode along Uncle kept seeing towers that were quite new to him. Water cascaded in channels down the walls of some towers from lakes that were on the top. The water came foaming down into the moat, often through the mouths of great stone gargoyles. There were orchards to be seen by the water, and the moat was full of fish. Far away, on one distant tower, there seemed to be a show of some kind, for tiny flags were flying. Most of the towers were bare, but one of them was covered to the top with pink roses, and another had small holly trees growing here and there all the way up. On some towers were tremendous golden shields, and many had great silver lamp-posts. Lion Tower, the highest of all, rose from the middle of a group of clustering towers, and on the edge of it, like a tiny upward pointing finger, stood a light-house. This was the home of Captain Walrus.

Uncle lay back in the carriage and pondered over the vast array of towers which made up his home.

"Shall I ever be able to get round to them all?" he wondered.

Gradually, travelling quietly through the fields, they came to the opposite side of the castle to that where Uncle lived. Not far ahead could be seen the banyan tree outside Colonel Lungy's bungalow, and beyond that the back of the Art Gallery.

A line of washing was hanging out between two windows of the Art Gallery, and a rather frayed rope ladder was hanging from another.

"We can't allow that," said Uncle. "I must have a word with Snowjuice."

Even as he spoke, Mrs Snowjuice was to be seen in the distance hastily gathering the washing in.

When they got round to the front of the Art Gallery, Snow-juice, looking quite smart in a clean white shirt and well-brushed cap, was waiting to admit them. Waldovenison Smeare appeared, looking much fatter, and holding a brush and palette.

"Well, how are things, Snowjuice?" asked Uncle.

"Oh, we're getting on well, sir," said Snowjuice. "Three visitors yesterday and three last Monday, and one of them gave me threepence towards the Founder's Fund. Here it is, sir."

"Thanks," said Uncle, pocketing the coin. "Though not a great deal it is a start. By the way, Snowjuice, it looks a bit shabby to hang washing out of the Art Gallery windows, and I don't much like the rope ladder. Who uses that?"

"I do, sir," said Waldovenison Smeare. "I'll remove it. I'm afraid I got into the habit when access was difficult from the front."

"Things are altogether better, sir," said Snowjuice. "All the rooms are in use now, and never a scream in the night – thanks to you."

"I'm bottling a lot of miserberries," said Mrs Snowjuice happily. "They come in useful during the winter, but I've never felt safe gathering them before."

"Long may this happy state of affairs last," said Uncle. "I'm doing my best to see that it does, and you must do all you can to keep things clean and cheerful for visitors."

"And how soon will come the glorious day when I can start on a full-length portrait of you, sir?" asked Smeare.

"I am much occupied at the moment, Smeare," said Uncle. "I will let you know. Meanwhile where is the One-Armed Badger? Let's all sit down and have some refreshments before we go to Crack House."

As the Respectable Horses hadn't seen the Old Masters, they all had lunch in the newly-cleaned gallery. Uncle looked at the pictures again. He liked them a bit better, but he still didn't like them much. The Respectable Horses said they particularly liked one which showed a small white horse in a large brown field. The horse reminded them, they said, of a distant cousin.

After lunch Uncle and the Respectable Horses crossed the stretch of green to Crack House. Will Shudder was anxious to have a closer look at the Old Masters, and Smeare said he would go round with him. The Old Monkey and Goodman were going to play snakes and ladders with the Snowjuice children in the newly done-up sitting-room, and the One-Armed Badger, having got rid of his big bale of eatables, said he would like a nap on the sofa.

The door at Crack House was slowly opened by an enormous lion dressed in a dark-green velvet uniform with plain gold buttons. No need to ask. This was Leominster.

"What is your pleasure, sir?" he asked in a loud roaring voice.

"I want to see Mr Smoothy, and these ladies have come to see you," said Uncle.

Leominster seemed to take no notice of the Respectable Horses, but answered gravely:

"I will tell Mr Smoothy that you are here, sir," and walked off.

"He seems very stiff," said Uncle.

"Oh, that's Leominster to a T," said Miss Anna. "He's all stiffness and starch, but we'll get him to unbend!"

Leominster came back and said:

"Mr Smoothy will be pleased to see you in the study, sir, and I am instructed to entertain your equine companions in my own sitting-room."

Leominster must have unbent quite a lot almost at once, for Uncle was hardly seated in Smoothy's study before the sound of grave leonine laughter mixed with high-pitched feminine neighing echoed down the passage.

"Glad you're here," said Smoothy, unlocking a drawer in his desk and producing a long tray of buns. "I'd have got Leominster to set out a proper lunch, but it takes him so long."

"Thank you, but I've already had lunch with my friends the

Respectable Horses and the staff of the Art Gallery," said Uncle.

"Oh, you must have something," said Smoothy. "These are Pigweed Truffle Buns, very satisfying, and here is a glass of home-made Dock Leaf Wine. Dockie I call it. People laugh, but I am a great believer in it. Dock leaf is good against nettle stings, we all know that, so why shouldn't it be good in the stomach? Answer me that, sir."

"It doesn't taste bad," said Uncle, sampling a glass.

While they chewed their way through a trayful of Pigweed Truffle Buns, Uncle inquired about the general state of things at Crack House.

"You'd have let me know if the odious Batty had returned," said Uncle.

"No signs yet, but I guess we can expect him the moment we start — "

Smoothy stopped speaking and came round the desk and whispered into Uncle's ear.

" — digging."

"What about using the word DLOG as a secret word instead of having to whisper?" said Uncle, who finds whispering tickles his ear.

"Sound notion," said Smoothy. "I like it. Let's start at once. The difficulty is how do we dlog without seeming to dlog?"

"I see A. B. Fox is outside," said Uncle. "Let's ask him what he thinks, and show him the parchment. He needs all the information he can get."

"Look at him," said Smoothy, glancing out of the window. "Seems to be watching the ducks, and all the time keeping an eye on Crack House. He really is a smart fellow."

They strolled out on to the grass, passing an open window as they went towards the pond.

Anna, Ann, and Annette were sitting neatly on a sofa each with a can of Mallow Brash – a delicacy much loved by horses – before her. Facing them sat Leominster in a large silver-mounted chair.

"He was carrying a plate of pheasant," Leominster was saying, "and I at once remonstrated: 'My Lord,' I said, 'allow me!' and I took the plate from him. I placed him between Colonel Rugby-Stubbs and the Honourable Ben Bar-Catcher —"

It was clear that Leominster and the Respectable Horses were having a very enjoyable time together.

A. B. Fox came strolling over the grass to meet them, and the ducks stopped crowding into the middle of the pond and looking anxious.

Uncle handed Fox the usual five shillings.

"Afternoon, Fox," he said. "We'd like a word with you and as we're in the open here there's no fear of being overheard. Mr Smoothy has the chief document in the case with him and would like your opinion on it."

Smoothy undid the ancient crackling parchment once more and Fox settled down on the grass to study it. He held it flat with his two front paws and looked very intelligent.

"That reads, 'Search ye aboute with ye long smalle snout for ye dlog!'" said Smoothy, helping him.

"Dlog is of course gold spelt backwards," said Fox.

Uncle was a bit disappointed at this swift understanding of the code word, but, after all, he told himself, it was Fox's job to see through things instantly. Most people would be completely mystified.

"So this creature Batty's got wind of the buried treasure," said Fox, going straight to the point. "That's what he's after!"

"We aim to use the word dlog from now on," said Smoothy, "for either treasure or digging. Agreed?"

"Some scheme needed to hide the fact you're dlogging," said Fox, rolling up the parchment. He added one brief word as he handed it back to Smoothy: "Trees."

"What d'you mean, trees?" said Uncle, glancing round.

There wasn't, of course, a tree in sight. Only a few miserberry bushes. Uncle doesn't like people who talk too much, but sometimes he felt Fox didn't talk enough.

"Plant 'em," said Fox, "all round Crack House. You have to dlog good big holes to plant trees."

Uncle and Smoothy looked at each other in amazement. The simple brilliance of this plan stunned them. They had been racking their joint brains to think how things could get moving without arousing the suspicions of Batty, and Fox had shown them the way in a second.

Uncle handed him an extra shilling and Smoothy insisted on taking him back to Crack House for a plate of Pigweed Truffle Buns.

"Woeband's been sulking ever since Leominster arrived," said Smoothy. "I guess he's jealous. I'll get him going on this dlogging stunt. He's great on improving the property."

"Get the Snowjuice children to dlog," said Fox. "A lot of kids about with small spades would put Batty off."

Smoothy smote A. B. Fox on the back.

"You're real smart, aren't you?" he cried.

"Butterskin Mute's the best nursery gardener in these parts," said Uncle. "He'll supply you with saplings."

"Platchwiggins are too much to hope for, I guess," said Smoothy.

"And what are platchwiggins?" asked Uncle.

"Trees with fearfully long roots," said Smoothy. "They need great deep holes dug for them."

"Just what you want," said Uncle.

"I'll ride over at once and see this man Mute," said Smoothy.

The Respectable Horses were busy each putting a few lines in Leominster's album, but at last Leominster bowed them out on to the steps. As he did so he lifted his tail and curled it round, and, without for a moment losing his decorous butler's attitude, flicked a small piece of mud off one of Uncle's boots."

"That means you're all right with Leo," said Smoothy delightedly, as he accompanied Uncle to the carriage. "He only does that for people he thinks highly of."

They all had a pleasant ride home with only one deplorable incident to mar the peace.

They were passing under a rustic bridge over which tumbled masses of roses, and Uncle, reclining majestically in the coach, had his trunk upraised to inhale the scent of the flowers, when a hideous face appeared between two dirty feet, just above their heads.

Beaver Hateman peered down at them. He was sitting on the bridge with his feet dangling right amongst the roses. He doesn't worry about thorns, his skin is too thick.

"Lying there, you big barrel of lard!" he shouted. "Pulled by those stiff-jointed slaves!" Then he put on an unnaturally posh voice. "Tea at Crack House with Mr Smoothy! Hand round the Pigweed Truffle Buns and Dockie, Leominster!"

The Respectable Horses put on an extra spurt and Hateman was soon left behind. Nobody made much of this foul insult. It was beneath contempt. All the same Uncle was a little worried.

Beaver Hateman, by some means or other, knew exactly where he had been and what he had been doing. A close watch was being kept on Crack House. That much was clear.

The Old Monkey Has a Good Idea

BUTTERSKIN MUTE came to see Uncle a day or two after this. He was wearing a new smock and had a big basket of melons with him.

"Hello, Mute," said Uncle. "Have some Koolvat."

Mute put his rake in a corner and accepted a large mug of the refreshing drink.

"A fine tree the platchwiggin, sir," Mute said at last, wiping his mouth on his sleeve. "Roots as long as rivers they 'ave. Roots that's got to be spread out deep and proper."

"I gather Mr Smoothy has been to see you," said Uncle, "and that you've supplied him with young platchwiggins. That's fine, Mute, fine. I sent him to you, as a matter of fact."

"Proper good turn, sir. Never thought to get rid of the lot like that. So I went and bought meself a new smock."

"I thought Mute was looking very smart, didn't you?" Uncle said, turning to the Old Monkey.

"Very smart indeed, sir," said the Old Monkey, smiling.

"Feels a bit stiff like," said Mute, "but it'll wear comfortable with some mud on it."

Uncle sent Mute to the pantry with the Old Monkey to have some nut-and-honey ice-cream which he specially likes.

As soon as he had gone Uncle rang up Smoothy.

"Glad to hear Mute had a supply of platchwiggins," he said.

"I'm getting started at once with the planting!" shouted Smoothy in a delighted voice. "Any hope of sending a dlogging party?"

"We might make one up," said Uncle. "Things seem fairly quiet at the moment."

"Come along as soon as you can then, and we'll have a late unch in my great greenhouse. What d'you say?"

"Capital," said Uncle.

"Bring spades," said Smoothy.

Uncle rang up Cowgill's Works and asked Cowgill to produce a bundle of new spades from the tool store.

Cloutman and Gubbins, the Old Monkey and Whitebeard were rounded up. The One-Armed Badger brought some provisions and ointment in case they cut themselves. Butterskin Mute asked if he could come as he was most anxious to show Smoothy how to spread out the platchwiggin roots properly.

Goodman was yawning a good deal but still wanted to come.

"You look very sleepy, Goodman," said Uncle. "What's the matter?"

"I was up most of the night with Mr Fox," he said.

"Any developments?" asked Uncle.

"Mr Fox will tell you," said Goodman, mysteriously.

"Oughtn't we to ask Captain Walrus to keep a sharp look-out, sir?" said the Old Monkey. "If Hateman had any idea so many of us were going to be away from home he'd be up here in a flash."

This was a solemn thought.

"You're quite right," said Uncle.

"Can I help?" asked Will Shudder. "I'm not much of a dlogger, sir, but if Captain Walrus and myself kept alternate watch here we could get help at once if anything suspicious occurred."

"Good idea, Shudder. I'll ring Walrus and ask him to take the express lift," said Uncle.

He told everybody else to get ready quietly, and not to drop spades on the stone steps as they started for Crack House or otherwise arouse the suspicions of any spies from Badfort who might be about.

Tabby Bismuth, who was knitting an immensely long scarf

for one of her grandchildren, opened the door in the cupboard promptly.

"Morning all," she said cheerfully, and offered everybody a humbug from a bag labelled: *Cheapman's Store – ½d. for 300 Humdinger Humbugs.*

What a scene of activity there was at Crack House.

Piles of platchwiggin saplings, their long roots coiling like cables, lay on the grass, and close to the house itself were mounds of freshly dug earth.

All the Snowjuice children were standing up to their eyebrows in deep holes, and Smeare was languidly throwing up a few clods with a coal shovel. Woeband, wearing only a striped jersey and red trousers, was sweating a lot as he dug. Smoothy, looking very wiry in shorts, a checked shirt and an eye-shade, jumped out of a deep hole to greet Uncle's party.

"How's this for action!" he shouted, and winked at Uncle.

The spades were soon distributed. Most of Uncle's party took off their shirts because it was very hot in that enclosed space between the great towers.

"We'll cover every inch this way," said Smoothy to Uncle. "If there's any dlog to be found we'll find it."

"Is Fox about?" asked Uncle.

"Saw him not long ago," said Smoothy. "He's not dlogging, of course, as he's keeping a sharp look-out as usual."

"Well, I'm not much good at spade work," said Uncle, "but in what way can I help? Lifting buckets of earth, or pushing earth down on to roots? I think you should plant a platchwiggin or two just for the look of the thing."

"And I hope they grow," said Smoothy. "We could do with some trees around here."

He mopped himself with a large red-and-yellow handkerchief. Butterskin Mute took charge of the planting. He insisted on

spreading out the roots of the saplings very, very carefully, and very, very slowly.

Uncle was getting hot, and he thought Fox was pretty wily just gliding about keeping an eye on things. Just as he was reluctantly curling his trunk round the handle of a bucket of earth, Fox appeared by his side.

"A word with you, sir," he said.

Uncle gladly dropped the bucket and walked with Fox to the middle of the grassy space where nobody could overhear them. Woeband looked out of a hole as they passed.

"Some people knows how to fix things, don't they?" he said, staring at Fox. "Never a hair out of place, and the same goes for that lazy lump Leominster. Too grand to dlog, he is! Keeps isself nice and cool, don't he?"

Uncle had a bit of sympathy with Woeband's outburst, for it was irritating, when all were hot and tired, to see Fox looking so cool and Leominster doing nothing except stand in the doorway of Crack House looking dignified.

"Told you Batty would come back. Well, he did, last night," said Fox, accepting the usual five shillings from Uncle.

"This is grave news," said Uncle.

"Leominster dealt with him," said Fox. "Afraid I can't take any credit."

"Leominster?" Uncle was astonished.

"Goodman will tell you," said Fox, who hates talking as much as Goodman likes it. He gave a sharp bark and Goodman looked out of a hole, happily dropped his spade and came scampering over the grass towards them.

"Oh sir," he said, "I must tell you about last night! Leominster was wonderful! You wouldn't think to look at him now that he could move over the grass like a thunderbolt, would you?"

"No, I don't think I would," said Uncle, looking at Leominster, who was gracefully swinging his tail to keep passing flies and mosquitoes away from him.

"Mr Fox and I were sitting under the miserberry bushes," said Goodman, "keeping an eye on Crack House. All of a sudden there was Batty, gliding down over the towers, his lilac eyes sort of swimming and glowing. Mr Fox whipped out his pest-pistol — "

"But monster out of range," said Fox.

"We crept from bush to bush, to get nearer to Batty without his seeing us," went on Goodman. "He was hopping along the tops of the mounds of earth and peering into the holes. Soon he got to the crack, and we thought he was going to fly up into it. Then, suddenly, the door of Crack House opened and Leominster was there. You know how stately he is, sir? Well, he stepped in a very dignified way towards Batty and said in a loud roaring voice: 'May I ask what you are doing in this area at this time of night?' "

"Good question," said Uncle.

"Batty gave a horrible sort of squeaky scream, flapped his wings and shook his folded fists at Leominster. Then he screeched, 'Mind your own business, you old stuffed shirt!' When he heard that, Leominster turned from being a butler into a furious lion. He leaped after Batty, and beat him with blow after blow of his paws. Batty couldn't get off the ground at first, but at last he managed it and went and sat on the roof of Crack House to get his breath back and then flew slowly off, sort of creaking and moaning."

"I'm a bit relieved to hear this," said Uncle. "I was rather afraid Leominster was going to be too stiff and starched for rough work."

"Oh no, sir, he's splendid!" cried Goodman. "You needn't worry! Once roused he's terrible!"

"Glad he's on our side," said Fox. "That's all I can say."

Uncle thanked Goodman for telling the story and sent him back to the digging.

"Must set a good example, you know," he said.

Goodman sighed heavily and went back very slowly.

"No hard feelings," said Fox, "but Butterskin Mute's a nuisance. Look, he's got half the dloggers fetching water for the platchwiggins. We're never going to get the ground round Crack House dug up at this rate!"

"You're right," said Uncle. "Wish I could think of a way of hurrying things up without giving away what we're really doing."

He paced to and fro, thinking hard, and while he was doing this the Old Monkey jumped out of one of the holes and came to look for him. Uncle tells the Old Monkey everything, so he knew that the planting of the platchwiggins was only a cover for the treasure hunt.

"Sir," he said, "I've got a good idea."

"Let's have it then," said Uncle.

"What about your buried-treasure detector – the one Whitebeard gave you?"

Uncle looked puzzled.

"You remember! On the day we went to Owl Springs."

"Thank you, what a brilliant idea!" cried Uncle and turned to Fox, clapping him on the back. "Fox, we have it! The Old Monkey has thought of a solution!" he cried.

Fox allowed himself to collapse on the grass in a way he had learned in his judo classes, so Uncle's friendly blow did not hurt him. Now he shook himself and stood up.

"If Whitebeard gave it to you it can't be much good," he said.

"He didn't realize at all what it was. He thought it was just an old medal he'd picked up in the street. He gave it to me for my birthday," said Uncle.

"And it turned blue when you stood on a mound of earth and under the surface were nine half-crowns in grease-proof paper!" cried the Old Monkey.

"Perfectly correct," said Uncle. "We found it turned blue the moment there was metal directly beneath it. I keep it locked up. I don't need any treasure myself and if I had it lying about Whitebeard would always be borrowing it. Look here, this might be the way out of all our difficulties."

"Might be," said Fox.

"I'll give you a note to Will Shudder," said Uncle, "and he can get it for you. While the rest of us are looking round the great greenhouse with Mr Smoothy you can test the earth round Crack House."

"Right," said Fox.

The Old Monkey returned very happily to the digging, for there is nothing that gives him so much pleasure as helping Uncle.

As Uncle passed the diggers on his way to write the note to Shudder, he told Smoothy what he intended to do.

"Good," said Smoothy. "Time we had a break. Troops are getting restless. Let's call a halt and go to the greenhouse."

"Good notion," said Uncle.

He hastily wrote a note to Will Shudder which read:

Take key with red label from bunch 1067598436 and unlock stinkwood cupboard in north bay of library. Give to the bearer of this letter, A. B. Fox, small parcel wrapped in silver paper and marked Most Secret.

"Good," said Uncle, "I feel some progress is being made. And now we deserve some time off, I think. Let's have a look at this greenhouse of yours. Where can it be? That's what puzzles me."

"Ah," said Smoothy, "you'll soon see!"

FIFTEEN

The Great Greenhouse

THE hot band of diggers were soon assembled, and they set off for a small door in the tower behind Crack House. It had a knocker shaped like a hammer.

"Give it a good knock," said Smoothy to Uncle.

Uncle did. A very good knock indeed, but nothing happened. Smoothy laughed, and so did Woeband.

"Just one of Mr Smoothy's little tricks," said Woeband.

"When you have finished laughing perhaps you will show me how to do it," said Uncle.

"You just knock and press on the foot-scraper at the same time," said Smoothy.

Uncle was feeling too hot to appreciate jokes. However, he did what Smoothy said and the door opened at once. At the end of a short passage was a glass door. When they opened this they were in the great greenhouse.

It was an immense place – more like a huge glass-roofed field – extending from one tower to another. There were palm trees and tropical plants everywhere, and in the middle was a gigantic pool, almost like a lake. Banyan trees, cedars and flowering shrubs were growing thickly enough to make a forest and there were even monkeys in the trees and a few leopards moving smoothly around.

"I say," said Uncle to Smoothy, "it must cost you a packet to heat this place!"

"Oh no," said Smoothy, "I just put in pipes which are heated by thousand-year oil. Once started, the thing runs on."

Some monkeys were beginning a long dive together, and this was too much for the Old Monkey.

"Oh sir, could I have a swing with them? I won't be long!"

Uncle nodded, and the Old Monkey flung himself upwards on to a branch and screamed and chattered as he had done when he was young.

Smoothy laughed.

"And that reminds me. There's a fine grove of coconuts and sugar-canes over there. You can have some real sugar-cane for dessert today."

Uncle and Smoothy had their meal at a stone table by the lakeside. Leominster was there to wait on them, but the others had a more informal feast with the One-Armed among the palm trees.

Leominster was dressed in his heavy black waiter's suit and stiffly starched shirt, and made the meal as formal as he could. It wasn't easy for there were so many fishes about.

The fishes in the lake seemed to know Smoothy, and looked to him for food. One fish actually took a flying leap in the air, seized some meat from Smoothy's plate, and with a tremendous swing of the tail got back into the water. This happened more than once, until the table was pretty well cleared.

Leominster looked on with a pained expression, and while Smoothy was throwing the last scraps into the lake he took away the cloth and asked:

"Is there anything else, sir?"

"No, thanks," said Smoothy, "but one thing, why don't you take off that shirt and suit and just be an ordinary lion for a bit? Do you good!"

Leominster looked shocked at first, and then suddenly smiled, threw off his hot black suit, and with a great roar rushed into the forest where they could hear him prowling about and splintering trees.

"He likes to be just a lion every now and again, though he pretends not to. And now what about a chew among the sugar-canes for you! I'm going to have a swim. I love the fishes. People think I come to catch them, but I really just like playing with them!"

"Are these the fishes you came to see the day you fixed poor Lungy to the couch?" asked Uncle rather sternly.

"Who told you about that?" asked Smoothy, looking a bit ashamed.

"Woeband," said Uncle.

"That fellow talks too much," said Smoothy, and added: "It was a bit rough, I grant you. I must ride over on my motor-bike and listen to one of his stories – right through to the end – by way of apology."

"You do that," said Uncle.

Smoothy had bathing trunks under his suit and he soon undressed and plunged into the lake. Uncle walked over to the sugar-canes which were fresh and crisp. He had a good munch.

When he got back to the lake he watched Smoothy playing among the fishes. Smoothy can swim almost as fast as a fish. He was having a sort of race with one big blue fish which was about five feet long. He was losing, so he caught hold of the fish's tail and it pulled him along. Then he got alongside the fish by catching hold of a fin, and pretended the race had ended in a draw. When the race was over he gave the fish a playful smack on the head, and the fish seemed to know it was fun and gave him a pretend bite on the arm.

When Smoothy got out all the fishes gathered into what looked like a solid block of fish. He lifted his hands as if he was going to throw them some food and then dived right into the middle of the swirling fish. He surprised them, but did not frighten them, for when he surfaced they were in a solid ring round him. It's not easy to imagine a fish laughing, but their vacant faces somehow seemed to be slightly amused, and Uncle couldn't help smiling too. Smoothy called out:

"I tell you what, there's a big mud wallow on the other side of the lake reserved specially for elephants. Why not have a good wallow?"

Uncle, in spite of his honours and high offices, is terribly fond of wallowing in mud. He simply cannot resist it. So he slipped off his great walking gown, went to the edge of the lake and made a splendid dive. The splash scattered the fishes for many yards around. Then he surfaced and with loud majestic trumpeting swam steadily across the pool like a great steamer. Arriving at the other side he found the water full of the muddy ooze he loved. Here he lay and wallowed for a long time, and at last swam slowly back.

"A delightful and refreshing experience, Smoothy," he said.

"Glad you found it so," said Smoothy. "Would you mind calling up the Old Monkey and telling him that each member of the party is to get as many coconuts, mangoes and dates as he can carry home?"

While the party were busy with this joyous work of gathering, Smoothy and Uncle had a short but very serious talk.

"I'm glad we've had this hour or two off," said Smoothy, "for things are not looking too good at Crack House, and I'm pretty sure there is a big plot boiling up against you, sir. For instance, I found this speared to a platchwiggin tree last night. No point in showing it to Fox. It would depress him, and he's doing his best."

He showed Uncle a dirty piece of paper on which was scribbled in red: A. B. FOX FOXED AGAIN.

"Ah well," said Uncle, "they have to throw a poisoned dart or two, and maybe when we get back Fox will have located the treasure with my detector and we will have a straight course."

"Meanwhile we must redouble our watchfulness and be always on the alert," said Smoothy earnestly. "We can talk pretty freely in this quiet spot, I'm glad to say."

As he said this, Uncle noticed something strange about the surface of the lake water. It was pretty lively with fish, but what he saw was something different. It looked remarkably like a book travelling well above water-level and held by an unseen hand.

"It's as well you spoke," said Uncle, "for even at this moment we are observed."

"Where? Who? What?" asked Smoothy, turning round and round rapidly.

"Hitmouse, the wretched reporter and spy from the *Badfort News*, is swimming towards us underwater," said Uncle quietly. "He always holds his hating book up to keep it dry. He is one of the vilest of Hateman's crew. Just go on talking trivialities."

The small book advanced towards them, and they pretended

not to see the wretched Hitmouse reach the shelter of the bank and get one ear out of the water in order to listen.

Smoothy started talking in an extra loud, rasping voice.

"Book travelling on water. Right. Held by hand. Right. Body under bank now. Right. Body belongs to miserable skewer-poker Hitmouse. Right – Right – Right!"

The water below the bank seemed to boil, Hitmouse was so angry. He surfaced, and while still holding the book above water with one hand somehow got a skewer in the other and threw it at Smoothy.

As he did so, Uncle reached down with his trunk, tore the hating book out of Hitmouse's other hand and threw it right across the water into the ooze of the bank.

The skewer missed and Hitmouse paddled across the lake like a torpedo. He was too late, of course, to save his precious book from falling into the mud, but when he saw its pages streaming with watery black slime he gave a small but very terrible scream. Then, howling and bubbling, he disappeared among the trees.

"Well done," said Smoothy. "Never saw anything neater!"

"Certainly it was an act of justice," said Uncle. "That hating book is a vile and infamous thing."

"But how did the little beast get into my great greenhouse?" Smoothy wondered. "Just how?"

It was a disturbing thought. There seemed no place entirely free from the Badfort crowd.

And when they got back to Crack House a great disappointment awaited them.

Uncle, Smoothy and Fox had a short conference apart from the others.

Fox had been unable to get any response out of the buried-treasure detector.

"Walked round Crack House five times, and never a hint of

blue," he said. "It's working all right because I put my daily five bob under a mound of earth and then stepped on it. Enough blue to make a pair of sailor's trousers. I'm afraid we've drawn a complete blank. There isn't any treasure buried near Crack House."

This was rather a set-back. If the treasure was not buried in the ground near Crack House, where was it? Until it was found they would never get rid of Batty.

"I'll keep the detector for the night," said Fox to Uncle. "I'll cover every inch again, just to make sure."

"And I'll stay behind with Mr Fox for a bit, if you don't mind, sir," said Goodman running up to them.

The rest of the party set off for home laden with fruit and nuts. The One-Armed had piled up an immense pack of coconuts, and was quite invisible under them and perfectly happy.

SIXTEEN

Discovery at Crack House

DARKNESS falls quickly among the vast towers of Homeward, and it was necessary to get across Quack Walk while there was still some light, so before long Fox and Goodman found themselves alone outside Crack House.

All the lights had gone out at the Art Gallery. Waldovenison Smeare had offered to come and play the guitar to them, but Fox thought it would take their minds off their work, so he had gone back to his shed at the back of the Art Gallery. Leominster had locked up Crack House for the night. Only the ducks were awake, for they knew Fox was near and hesitated to huddle near the banks and doze off as they usually did.

"Let's get started then," said Fox to Goodman. "Noses down and we must cover every inch."

"Right, Mr Fox," said Goodman, licking the buried-treasure detector and then polishing it with his paw.

They were just about to start off when the door of Crack House opened. Smoothy, in a red dressing-gown embroidered with golden dragons, stood there and called:

"Hi, Fox, I'm off to bed, but I'll put the key of Crack House under the mat in case you want to call me. My room's the one with the electric frog on the door. It'll croak loudly when you touch it. Leominster has a few snacks to keep you going. Good hunting."

"May good fortune attend your searches," said Leominster, and put on the bottom step a tray of Pigweed Truffle Buns, a flask of Dockie and a bowl of milk.

Fox sighed. These things weren't exactly his idea of a good midnight snack.

"You can have half the milk," said Goodman.

Then followed some wearisome hours of slow loping round Crack House. Sometimes Goodman held the buried-treasure detector between his teeth and sometimes Fox held it. They

worked side by side, so that if the faintest glimmer of blue showed the one who was not holding the medal would see it. But there was never a glimmer.

As it was summer the dawn came early, and at last, in the first faint glow of rosy light, Fox stopped his slow nose-to-ground forward movement and dropped the buried-treasure detector. He looked at Goodman. Goodman's nose is usually beautifully clean, but now it was covered with earth and his tail was drooping. They looked very tired.

"Goodman," said Fox, "the parchment said, 'Snuffle around with ye nose to ye ground — ' "

"Yes, it did," said Goodman, yawning.

"Whoever wrote that was trying to put buried-treasure hunters off, I guess. We must start again."

"Oh, no!" cried Goodman. "I can't bear it. Start again! Oh, Mr Fox, we just can't!"

Goodman sneezed and shivered. The dawn wind was very chilly.

"We can and will," said Fox, "inside Crack House."

"Inside! But it says ground, and ground is outside!"

"That's what I mean. It's a false trail. I've got a hunch that we should try inside."

So they got the big old key out from under the mat, and with cold stiff paws struggled to get the door open. At last they managed it. The hall was dark and silent, and very warm after the cold outside.

"Where's the detector?" asked Fox.

Goodman had left it by the bowl of milk. He hurried back down the steps to fetch it.

Fox took it. Not a glimmer of blue.

Then he stepped into the hall.

At once the whole shadowy hall was lit by a strong flashing blue light from the detector.

"Oh, Mr Fox," cried Goodman, "you were right! There must be buried treasure here, exactly here, just inside the front door! What a funny place!"

Then Fox moved further into the hall, and the light went on flashing.

"It's not just inside the door, it's everywhere!" cried Goodman. "Absolutely everywhere."

They ran about from room to room after that, and the detector went on flashing, flashing, flashing.

"There's treasure spread out under the whole floor of Crack House!" cried Goodman. "But what's the good of just knowing that. How can we get to it!"

"Down to nose-work again," said Fox. "Nothing else for it. There must be some secret spring somewhere that shows the way. We must cover every inch of this place."

"My nose will wear out soon," said Goodman. "It feels very thin in places now."

Wearily Fox and Goodman sniffed and felt their way over the hall, library and drawing-room. It was fearfully tiring work feeling over all the furniture and floorboards.

"And the dining-room's the worst of the lot," sighed Goodman. "All that carved oak. It'll take hours!"

The big carved table in the centre of the dining-room floor was ornamented with a very complicated pattern of leaves, flowers and fruit.

"Oh, I hate all this carved oak!" groaned Goodman, feeling round a very complicated set of carved oak leaves and acorns.

"Keep going!" said Fox, squatting down by the fourth leg of

the dining-table. "These legs are fixed into the tiles, you know. That's pretty unusual."

"The whole place is unusual, and, to tell the truth, Mr Fox, I don't think we're getting anywhere!"

"That's four o'clock in the morning talk," said Fox. "Let's have no more! . . . Hullo! That gave when I touched it!"

Almost as he spoke there was a creaking rumbling sound. The whole table tilted sideways and a square opening in the tiled floor showed just beside them. The top of the trap-door was a neat oblong of tiles backed with metal and with the four legs of the table embedded in the four corners. This oblong had fitted so neatly into the pattern of the tiles that there had not been the smallest trace of it.

Goodman and Fox leaned over to look down into the hole, and saw a short flight of stone steps, thick with powdery dust and spider webs. Below that they could make out some dim and dusty shapes of what looked like large logs.

"But where's the treasure?" said Goodman, sadly. "Don't say we've got to do any more searching! There aren't any jewels or gold coins here! You can see that!"

"Call the boss," said Fox.

Goodman rushed up the stairs and put his paw on the electric frog which was fixed to the middle of Smoothy's bedroom door. At once a hideous croaking started, and very soon Smoothy opened the door.

"Well?" he said. "Any luck?"

"We don't know," said Goodman, "but we've found a secret room under the dining-room floor. Come and look, Mr Smoothy, and if you've got a torch it would help."

"This one works on thousand-year oil," said Smoothy, taking a torch about as big as a fire-extinguisher from a hook inside his bedroom. "Cuts out all that fooling about with batteries."

Soon Smoothy, Fox and Goodman were peering into the gloomy dust-shrouded depths below the dining-room.

"Seems to be circular." said Smoothy. "Well, what about it, lads?"

"I'll go first," said Fox.

It was most unpleasant to go down those steps with cobwebs shifting across their faces and clinging to their ears. The dust was almost as thick and clogging as desert sand.

"Hundreds of years this must have been lying here," said Smoothy. "Just the sort of place Batty would like."

The thousand-year-oil torch threw a powerful beam among the lumpy shapes which had looked like logs from above. These turned out to be strong rough tables and chairs made from un-shaped sections of huge tree-trunks. Here and there were signs of sawn-off branches on the sides of the rough furniture. But there was nothing else in the low-roofed circular room except two small holes near the roof which appeared to be rough ventilators.

"How come we didn't notice those holes outside?" asked Smoothy, training his torch on to one of them. Nothing could be seen but more cobwebs and dried leaves and a few sticks.

"I did notice them, but I thought they were part of the ground floor," said Fox.

"Well, there's no sign of treasure," said Smoothy.

"It's here," said Fox, "right here, somewhere. Detector says so."

"Let's get out," said Smoothy. "I'll get Woeband and my double-suction giant vacuum cleaner to suck up this dust. Then we'll have another look. You boys had better have a good kip while the cleaning goes on."

They all three felt rather depressed as they went up the steps. To start again was a dismal prospect. Goodman sneezed so violently that he missed his footing and slithered down the steps in a cloud of dust to land on the floor of the circular room.

"Bad luck," said Smoothy. "Not hurt, are you?"

"No," said Goodman, sneezing again. "It's only this foul dust. I'll be glad to get out of here."

He scampered up the stairs and shook himself so violently that a small dust-storm seemed to be travelling over the tiled floor of the dining-room.

"Hi, do that outside!" said Smoothy.

"Look at this," said Fox, sharply. He had not left the trap-door, but was peering down the steps again and holding Smoothy's torch so that it shone on the floor of the secret room.

"What?" asked Smoothy.

"Look, there where Goodman fell," said Fox.

The torch showed their footprints and also the cleared patch where Goodman's falling body had cleared a wider space of dust. This space shone now in the light of the torch with a peculiarly lovely and glowing yellow.

"Floor's not made of stone then," said Smoothy.

Fox went quietly down the steps, and cleared a further space. The soft yellow glow of the floor shone up whenever the dust was cleared.

"What is it?" asked Smoothy in a puzzled voice. "What can it be?"

"It's gold," said Fox. "The whole floor is gold. Crack House is built upon a solid block of gold."

"Can't be!" muttered Smoothy, but he bent to the floor again.

"Might as well face it," said Fox. "I know gold when I see it. We've found the treasure."

SEVENTEEN

The Gold Block

"Where's Goodman?" asked Uncle at breakfast that morning. He missed the cat, who always brought the morning paper to him.

"He hasn't been home all night, sir," said the Old Monkey.

"Goodman mustn't have too many of these all-night sessions with Fox," said Uncle, "or he won't be fit for his ordinary duties. Shudder tells me there are a lot of parcels waiting to be wrapped up."

Uncle had hardly finished his first bucket of cocoa before Smoothy rang up.

"Splendid news, splendid!" he shouted. "What a clever chap Fox is! Can't talk now in case wire is being tapped. How soon can you get here?"

"As soon as I've seen Heffo, the postman, and had another bucket of cocoa," said Uncle. "Found any dlog?"

"Dlog!" shouted Smoothy. "Just you wait! Bring all the lads!"

Uncle finished his breakfast in a joyous hurry. An end to the difficulties at Crack House seemed in sight. To tell the truth, he was thankful that the planting of platchwiggan trees hadn't lasted too long. It had been a good idea but the weather was too warm for it.

When they got to Crack House, Leominster opened the door for them. He was dressed in a magnificent uniform of red and gold.

"A repast has been prepared for you, sir," he said, "in the Circular Lounge."

This was the first surprise. Crack House isn't big and they had been pretty well all over it! Where on earth could the Circular Lounge be?

Leominster led them with slow dignified steps to the dining-room, and there Smoothy, A. B. Fox and Goodman were waiting All of them were smiling mysteriously.

Goodman rushed up to Uncle.

"Oh, sir, I'm sorry I didn't help with the post and the news-papers this morning, but I just had to stay with Mr Fox. We nearly gave up, and then, well, Mr Fox solved the whole thing! I knew he would! I knew it. Didn't I say, right at the start, that Mr Fox was the best man for the job?"

"You did, Goodman," said Uncle, "and now, Fox, here's your usual five shillings."

"Pleased to report success," said Fox and saluted gravely.

Then he held up the buried-treasure detector.

"Oh, sir," gasped the Old Monkey. "Look, it's bright, bright blue!"

All the disappointment the Old Monkey had felt about his great inspiration having no good result vanished. The medal was flashing a strong blue light, almost as bright as the light on a police car.

Smoothy unfolded the Crack House parchment and said in his loud voice:

"I will read out the ancient instructions for finding the treasure. This is *all*, friends, that A. B. Fox had to go on. Please remember that.

> "Syt ye no more by ye fyre in ye halle
>   like ye hogge
> But search ye aboute with ye long smalle snout
>   for ye dlog
> Not to ye sky shall ye turne uppe ye eye
>   but like dogge
> Snuffle around with ye nose to ye ground
>   for ye dlog."

"You'll admit, sir," said Fox to Uncle, "that the word 'ground' usually means 'earth'. That's what put me off."

K

Then Fox did something surprising. He took the buried-treasure detector between his teeth and started to lope gracefully round the room, starting at the wall edge and coming in closer and closer to the table in the middle. It was delightful to watch. His coat and big tail were such a bright brown and the medal such a lovely flashing blue. And the coat and the tail and the blue light were all reflected and reflected back again in the wall mirrors.

Everybody clapped.

"Look, look!" cried the Old Monkey. "There must be treasure everywhere!"

Whitebeard had to sit down, he was so overpowered.

Smoothy laughed, delighted at the bewilderment of Uncle's party. Even Leominster, standing with his head in the air by the door, smiled a bit at the corners of his mouth.

Fox circled the big oak table twice, getting slower and slower till he stopped. Then he pressed with his paw on one of the carved legs.

At once there was the creaking, rumbling sound Fox and Goodman had heard before and as before the table tilted sideways. The oblong opening was there in the middle of the floor and everybody crowded to look into it.

"Neat, eh?" said Smoothy. "I asked the man I bought Crack House from why the table legs were set into the tiles like that, and he said he'd never known them any other way and it kept the table from slipping. All the time the arrangement was part of a secret entry to the treasure room."

"Well, what is the treasure?" asked Uncle. "How much gold is there?"

"Come and see," said Smoothy.

"Luncheon will be served in ten minutes, sir," said Leominster.

"You go down first, sir," said Smoothy to Uncle.

Soon Uncle's party was standing in the perfectly plain circular room under the floor of Crack House. The place was brilliantly lit by a single lamp set on the biggest of the tables in the middle of the room.

"That's thousand-year oil for you," said Smoothy. "Woeband and I ran a tube down from the kitchen. Then we could see to clean the place up."

"Well, it looks fine now," said Uncle, "and I'm very taken with these chairs and tables. They look immensely strong. But where is the treasure? I'm afraid I don't see any."

"Oh sir," cried Goodman, "look at the floor. Look at the floor, and keep on looking!" He skipped about, holding the buried-treasure detector.

"Can't you see, sir!" he shouted again.

"It appears to be made out of one mass of beautiful yellow metal," said Uncle. "Too soft and glowing for brass, not enough red in it for bronze — "

Whitebeard gasped and knelt down on the floor. "Oh rapture!" he said.

Uncle felt the almost velvety smoothness of the floor with the end of his trunk. The thought that flashed into his mind was so extraordinary he hesitated to speak.

"Can it be – can it possibly be gold?" he said at last.

"You've got it – it's dlog!" cried Smoothy. "Nothing but a solid block of gold. I drilled down six inches. Still gold. Crack House is built upon a block of gold! For all I know it may go down miles into the earth!"

They wandered about dazed for some minutes. Whitebeard just went on sitting on the floor, stroking it. It was clear that the builders of Crack House had done all they could to protect their treasure. The walls which circled the golden floor were of immense strength and thickness. Nobody could penetrate them without using bulldozers.

"I've asked Benjamin Cheapman to join us for a talk," said Smoothy, "as the treasure is of such immense value. *He* knows a lot about gold. We have a problem here. According to our agreement, we wish to share out whatever has been found, and do some good with it, but we never thought the treasure would be so vast."

"The responsibility is great," said Uncle. "We must give the matter deep thought."

When Cheapman arrived his astonishment was very gratifying to everybody. For once the financial expert was overwhelmed.

They all sat down to the splendid feast of coconuts, ham sandwiches, bananas, corned beef and biscuits that Leominster had provided. The One-Armed Badger had come with a comparatively small load of toffee-apples, nougat and chocolate-cream bars, realizing that Smoothy and Leominster would be offended if he brought too much. The sweets made a nice finish to the feast. Smoothy only had Seaweed Slashers, Dockie, and, as a small dessert, a Pigweed Truffle Bun.

Whitebeard asked if he could have lunch on the floor.

"Get up, Whitebeard," said Uncle sternly, "and take your proper place at the feast Mr Smoothy has provided."

"Oh please, sir," said Whitebeard, "may I be allowed to eat my food down here? I've sometimes dreamed of eating from a golden plate, sir, but to sit on a golden floor and eat – why, I may never have such a chance again!"

"Oh, I should let him," said Smoothy impatiently. "He'll be no good as company at the table – simply looking down at the floor all the time."

So Whitebeard was allowed to stay on the floor. They passed food down to him, but he didn't get as much as he would have done if he'd sat up to the table properly.

When everybody had finished Smoothy said to Uncle:

"Now, sir, will you open the discussion? What's the best thing to do about our find?"

Uncle rose majestically.

"I think," he said, "that to begin with we should coin gold pieces and give one to each person in the domain. It might bear the simple inscription on one side 'General Good', and have a picture of Homeward with the date on the other."

Most thought this a very good idea, but Benjamin Cheapman had something to say:

"If a coin was minted I think we should want a picture of the owner of Homeward on it. His good works are known to all."

Here deafening cheers interrupted him.

Uncle tapped on the table for silence.

"Thanks, friends," he said, "but I could not agree to have my picture on a coin unless a picture of Mr Smoothy was there too."

More cheers. Even Leominster gave such a leonine roar of HEAR-HEAR that it shook all the glasses and plates on the table.

This time Smoothy held up his hand for silence.

And then a very strange sound was heard.

It seemed to come from one of the small ventilators up near the ceiling.

Everybody turned to look.

They all sat quiet, listening.

The noise came again.

It was a mocking long-drawn-out whistle, repeated again and again.

Of course they all rushed to look closely at the ventilator, but they could only feel a draught and see nothing.

"Must just be the wind," said Smoothy. "Let's get on. We're eager for your advice, Mr Cheapman. What about giving a gold piece to everybody in this domain?"

"Well," said Cheapman, "I feel bound to tell you that the

distribution of so much gold would upset everything. Take my store, for instance. At present people get small wages, but I try to meet them, and I think you'll agree they don't do so badly. In my grocery department you can buy seven pounds of sugar for a halfpenny. What if somebody spent five shillings on sugar? My shelves would be empty. I have a very popular line of penny dresses for women! How many would be left if every woman had a pound to spend? What about my football boots for boys! I can now do them for a halfpenny a pair, but if every boy had a pound where would we be? This move would ruin me unless I put prices up and then nobody would be better off!"

At that moment a sort of shuffling was heard in the room above them.

"Sounds like trouble, Fox," said Uncle. "Have a look, will you?"

Fox leaped for the stairs, but as he reached them there was a horrible slithering sound and a strong smell, and Batty, lilac eyes,

frowsty wings, green beak and powerful folded fists, was upon
them. Everybody shrank back. At close quarters the monster was
quite awful.

However A. B. Fox moved forward.

"Get out!" he said.

But Batty stood there, just shrieking in a monotonous way, his
beak held ready to stab Fox if he moved.

Fox went steadily forward. Then, as he came within range of
the powerful beak, he suddenly jumped on to one of the small
strong tree-tables. Batty rushed at him, but Fox jumped aside
and the cruel beak sank deeply into the solid wood of the table.

For a moment Batty stood there raging and blubbering. The
table was so thick he was held fast by it. But although the great
beak was out of action he was in another way more dangerous
than before. He began to hop and half-fly round the room, making
a horrible simmering sound as though some vile pot was boiling.
Using the small strong table as a sort of battering ram, he charged
wildly about. Soon, in that small space, somebody was going to
be badly hurt. That was clear.

"Up the steps, everybody!" shouted Uncle. "Fox and I will
deal with this!"

The rest of the party scrambled up the steps while Fox and
Uncle drew Batty's attacks on to themselves.

Then Fox took out of his pouch a packet of Gleamhound's Den
Comfort For Pets.

The moment Batty saw this powder, which was such a powerful poison to him, he made a tremendous effort to free himself of
the table, bashing it on to the steps. But it was useless, so, bubbling
and raging, still held fast by the table, he scrambled up the steps
followed closely by Uncle and Fox.

Outside Batty made a last desperate effort to free himself. He
ran against one of the towers, at the same time making a double

screw-clutch with his powerful fists. There was a splintering sound and the table fell, split in two.

"Now for that great lump of an elephant and that poisoner Fox!" he screamed as he turned towards them.

The rest of the party, who had taken shelter in the trenches, shuddered as they saw the venom in the lilac eyes, and the way the great fists opened and shut like mechanical grabs. Mrs Snowjuice, who with the rest of the family was staring horrified out of the windows of the Art Gallery, screamed. Everybody expected A. B. Fox to be seized and crushed.

But Fox advanced coolly towards Batty and suddenly threw a whole handful of Den Comfort into his hideous face.

At once there was such a screaming that they all stopped their ears and cowered behind earth, rocks, walls and any available shelter.

As the noise became unbearable, with a final ear-splitting, bubbling yell Batty rose into the air and flew off towards Badfort.

"I'll be back!" he screamed. "Back, back, back, you vile poisoners!"

Everybody came out, a bit nervously, on to the grass.

"Just in time, Fox," said Uncle, gravely.

Everybody felt tired out after this, and Smoothy said he'd like to come back with Uncle to Homeward to talk things over – and also get away from the smell of bat for a time.

Whitebeard said he would sleep on the gold floor to keep watch with Woeband and Leominster until a council could be called. Somehow they had to decide what was to be done with the gold. Now that Batty had actually been in the underground room and seen the gold block, the Badfort crowd must know of it too. The responsibility, as Uncle had said, was great.

"I don't think I shall sleep at all," said Uncle, but his faithful friend, the Old Monkey, looked into the medicine cupboard and came back with a bottle.

"Try this, sir," he said. "It's Wake-Me-Up Mixture for Night Watchmen. It says on the label: 'Just take a spoonful and you won't sleep for eight hours.' "

Uncle took a spoonful, and almost at once began to look sleepy. The Old Monkey was soon rewarded by hearing his melodious snore, so he quietly took himself to bed as well.

EIGHTEEN

The Great Council

WHILE Uncle was preparing for the Great Council, at which it was to be decided how the gold block might be used, he had an unexpected visit from Dr Augustus Lyre, headmaster of the Select School for Young Gentlemen on Lion Tower. Uncle is one of the governors.

Dr Lyre brought with him his nephew who was called Arthur Lyre.

"I have come first, sir," he said, "to tell you of a great idea I have about the disposal of the gold block."

"I didn't realize this discovery was generally talked about," said Uncle, rather crossly, "but since you are here you might as well give me your views as you represent a number of parents."

"Before I do so," said Dr Lyre, "I wonder if you could have a word with Arthur? He has a great affliction. He seems compelled to tell lies. His surname being Lyre and his Christian name Arthur, the boys make fun of him. They call out: 'Ar-thur Lyre!' making it sound like 'Ah, the liar!' In my position this is very painful. I wondered if you could help him?"

"Well, there isn't much time before the Council, but I'll do what I can," said Uncle. He walked over to Arthur and said:

"How are you getting on, Arthur?"

"I do like to tell a lie now and then," said Arthur cheerfully.

"There you are!" cried Dr Lyre, in deep distress. "His very first sentence to you is a lie! He does *not* like to tell lies. He has told me so in his calmer moments."

"That's a lie, Uncle Augustus," said Arthur. "I enjoy telling a good lie, and I don't think you, Beaver Hateman, will do me any good."

"Oh, this is terrible! That's a monstrous lie!" wailed Dr Lyre. "Saying you are Beaver Hateman!"

Uncle went to his desk and brought out a packet of Gleamhound's Liar Lozenges.

"Now, Arthur," he said, "take one of these and you won't lie any more."

"Ha, ha!" said Arthur, his eyes shining as he looked at the bottle. "Those are Liar Lozenges. They will make me lie more and more. I'll take one. I *like* lying very much indeed!"

"These will help you," said Uncle.

Arthur swallowed a lozenge and then said in a calm and cheerful voice, "I'm sorry I called you Beaver Hateman, sir. No two people could be less alike."

Doctor Lyre gave a scream of joy.

"Oh, you've cured him! What a relief! This will go down in the 'Supplement to the History of Homeward' that I am just preparing! How can I thank you!"

"I'm glad to have helped," said Uncle. "Arthur, what about going outside to watch the fish in the moat while I talk to Dr Lyre. The Old Monkey can bring you a jug of Koolvat."

"Thank you, sir," said Arthur. "I love watching fish, and Koolvat is my favourite drink!"

And he quietly went out.

"He's speaking the *truth* again!" Doctor Lyre said exultantly. "Oh, it's a complete cure! Ordinarily he would have said he hated fish and Koolvat."

"Now what about your great idea?" asked Uncle.

Dr Lyre put a copy of his *History of Lion Tower* on the table. This has 11,567 pages in it, and the modern history section has a full description of Uncle opening the dwarfs' drinking fountains.

"Here, sir," he said, tapping the book, "I have a simple plan that will benefit everybody. Why not have a million copies of my great *History* printed and give one to each person? That would not upset the market."

"No," said Uncle, after considering this for a time, "it would certainly not upset the market, but it would upset the people. We want something that all would enjoy. A lot of these wolves and badgers can't read, you know, and the general opinion might be that you were making a profit for yourself."

"I only make a very little on each book," Dr Lyre pointed out.

"Yes, but it would add up to a great deal if you sold a million copies. No, Dr Lyre, I'm sorry, but I can't entertain the idea."

Dr Lyre looked very disappointed.

"It just struck me it might be a happy way out of your difficulties!" he said, sighing heavily.

After Lyre had gone they all set out for Crack House. The Great Council was to be held in the underground room and therefore on the gold block itself. It seemed the right place to hold it. Uncle had asked Cowgill because it was necessary to decide on some method of protecting the gold. If this was not done the Badfort crowd would never cease trying to get hold of it and there would still be no peace for anybody at Crack House.

Leominster had once again provided a first-class meal, and as soon as it was finished, and the table cleared, they sat down in the soft glowing light provided by the thousand-year-oil lamp, to try and find a solution to their great problem – how to share out the gold. It was rather surprising that there was no sign of A. B. Fox. Even Goodman did not know where he was.

Uncle took the chair this time and Smoothy spoke first.

"Well, sir," he said, "there's such a thing as thinking too much and getting no further. I'm for the original plan. A gold piece for everybody in the land."

"I must protest again, sir," said Cheapman. "The markets would be completely upset. I have warned you!"

At this moment there was a quick patter of steps on the stone staircase, and A. B. Fox, looking rather strange as his brilliant fur was smeared and streaked with whitewash, came rushing down the stairs. He swept off an old ragged muffler he had been wearing and went over to Uncle. His tongue was hanging out and he was panting.

"Your five shillings, Fox," said Uncle. "Sit down and calm yourself."

"Warning of danger, sir," he gasped. "Disguised as old road-sweeper – Bandy Fox – I've been lurking on edge of meeting held at Badfort."

"A meeting?" said Uncle, alarmed.

From long experience he knows that evil nearly always comes from a Badfort meeting.

"They know all about the gold block," said Fox, "and have already worked out a way to capture it."

"The scoundrels!" said Uncle.

"Plan to be put into operation at once. I ran here as fast as possible to warn you!"

"You've done well, Fox," said Uncle. "They may be marching from Badfort now!"

"I've brought a box of stone clubs here, sir," said Whitebeard. "I thought it best to have some by me while I was watching the gold floor."

"Good," said Uncle. "We are not altogether unprepared then. Fox, stay upstairs, and give us instant warning. Meanwhile, now we *are* gathered here, has anybody else any ideas?"

Suddenly the One-Armed Badger, who hardly ever speaks, climbed up on to one of the tree-tables. He held up his paw and said:

"To speak, sir."

"Well," said Uncle, looking kindly on his friend and helper, "what have you to say?"

"Please, sir, I think the best way to give everybody a share of gold is to give all a shilling every week when they come to pay rent."

L

Then he jumped off the table and sat down.

There was silence for a moment and then Uncle spoke.

"Friends," he said, "this humble friend has shown us a way. What do you say, Cheapman, as a financial expert?"

"It's quite the best idea we have had!" said Benjamin Cheapman.

"And," said Whitebeard, "you'll get in a lot of rents that would never be paid otherwise."

"Enough, Whitebeard," said Uncle. "That may be so, but it is not something to stress at the moment."

Everybody started to talk about the One-Armed Badger's plan and congratulate him on his brilliant idea. While they were doing this Smoothy handed round some trays of Pigweed Truffle Buns and Seaweed Slashers.

Goodman ran up the stairs once or twice, and came back to report that A. B. Fox had still seen no signs of the enemy, so they all felt reassured. Cowgill had been looking round the trenches already dug around Crack House for the platchwiggins, and suggested that an electric fence could be set up close around the walls of Crack House – perhaps buried in the ground. It need not be dangerous, but one touch of a tunnelling spade, or drill, would set off a hundred alarm bells on near-by towers.

They talked this over a bit, but it was very warm in the low-ceilinged room with so many people in it. Uncle felt they ought to break up the council so as to get outside.

"Warm, isn't it?" said Smoothy. "Wouldn't it be nice to have a swim in the great greenhouse lake?"

"Nothing I'd like better," said Uncle.

Smoothy yawned, and so did Leominster.

Uncle suddenly became aware that a change was coming over his followers.

Butterskin Mute put his rake on the table and said:

"I feel that sleepy, sir."

Cloutman, who had just been reaching for a ginger-nut, seemed to drop off even as he held his hand out.

Whitebeard, who had been affectionately lying on the gold block, began to snore. His snores vibrated his beard and showed the bag of food he had got stowed away under it.

The Old Monkey, who had just been going to take a drink from a glass of Koolvat, put it down and looked at his master with drowsy eyes.

"Oh, sir," he said piteously. "What's happening to us? I'm frightened!"

And even as he spoke he fell asleep.

Uncle himself was standing. He had been giving, after they had finished talking about the electric fence, a short speech on wise spending. But he was feeling increasingly drowsy.

Now he saw to his horror that he was the only person awake. What was happening? What unseen thing had caused all his followers to be reduced to helplessness?

His eyes ranged the low-roofed room desperately. Every second he felt more and more muzziness creep over him. He knew that the fate of everybody, now slumped heavily round the big table, depended on his not falling asleep himself.

He swayed on his feet. His eyelids felt like rocks.

And then, just as he felt he must collapse and give way to his terrible sleepiness, he saw a small rubber pipe sticking out an inch or two into the room from one of the small ventilators.

As he tried to focus his eyes on it, he saw that it was moving slightly up and down as if to the rhythm of some machine outside.

At once his mighty brain cleared away the descending fog.

Some kind of sleeping-gas was being pumped into the room!

Intense anger and sudden overwhelming fear gave him strength.

He leaped for the rubber tube and coiled his trunk round it, and pulled it as hard as he possibly could.

It fell into the room, and from the ventilator came a thin scream of rage.

Then Uncle looked more closely at the other ventilator. No fresh air was blowing from it, so he concluded it had been blocked from the outside. He needed something long and thin to push through one of the holes and break the covering away.

What could he possibly use?

Then he saw Butterskin Mute's rake, the rake he takes everywhere with him.

He seized it and pushed the handle through one of the holes in the ventilator, and at last, after pushing it almost to its limit, a cool draught of life-giving air poured into the room.

A sound behind him made him turn. To his horror the limp body of A. B. Fox was slithering down the stone staircase. Almost at once a great pair of feet appeared through the trap door, followed by a massive body in a sack suit. At last the hideous face of Beaver Hateman came into sight, half-hidden by a piece of sacking which he held over his nose and mouth to protect himself from the sleeping-gas.

"Here they are, boys!" he gave a raucous shout. "They're all weak as rats! The Dictator's here too, dopey as a poisoned pig! Come on, boys, we'll march the lot off to Badfort and tie 'em up. Then we can collar the gold in peace! Rivers of Black Tom, boys! Lakes of Leper Gin!"

Uncle managed to keep his eyes nearly closed, but as the air began to get fresher he felt his mind working more easily, and he was aware of the solid edge of the box of stone clubs which Whitebeard had spoken of near his side. He leaned stealthily down to grasp a club, and immediately felt strength return to him.

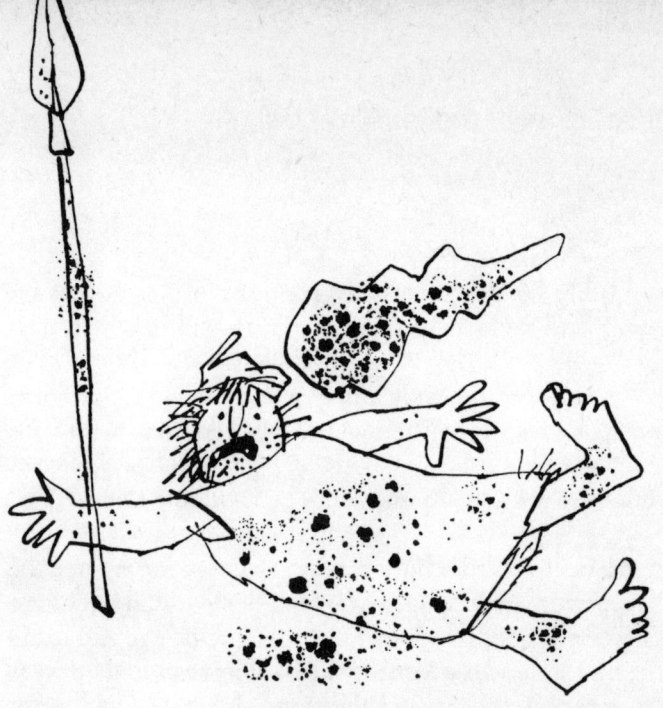

"Must have just one smack at the Big Bully," shouted Hateman, "while he's at my mercy!"

He raised his knotty arm and took aim with the boar-spear. As he did so, Uncle raised the stone club and quick as lightning hurled it at him.

At once Hateman was knocked flat and lay groaning on the steps.

There was a sound of confused shouting outside, coming nearer and nearer.

This meant that the Badfort crowd had arrived and were even now in the dining-room above.

The situation was desperate. With all his followers lying helpless how could Uncle hope to deal with so many alone? Once they surged down the stone steps the battle would be lost.

Even as he thought this Smoothy staggered to his feet.

"The Badfort crowd are already in the dining-room, Smoothy!" roared Uncle. "We've been gassed!"

"Leave it to me!" muttered Smoothy, and followed Uncle

rather unsteadily up the stone steps. He got a firmer grip as his head cleared, and said: "My thieves' mirror will deal with this rotten lot!"

In the dining-room he made a dive past the huge bluish form of Jellytussle, knocking Sigismund and Nailrod aside with yells of rage.

"Get out of my dining-room, you set of skulking thieves!" he yelled.

He must have touched a button near the door, for at once the walls all appeared to have archways in them leading to long corridors. This illusion, which had once taken Uncle in and made him bump his forehead, now made the Badfort crowd, who were seeking to escape Smoothy and the stone clubs of Uncle, crash helplessly against one wall after another. Blue strips of jelly floated from Jellytussle. Hootman was screaming in a thin ghostly way.

Between them Smoothy and Uncle got the whole battered and confused crowd driven at last through the one real door into the hall and out of the house.

"We must get back and fetch the others up!" gasped Uncle.

"Sure!" said Smoothy, turning with Uncle to the stone steps.

But they had no chance to go down them. Leominster had recovered now, and seeing Hateman crawling up the steps and trying to escape he gave a frightful roar.

Hateman limped as fast as he could across the dining-room but Leominster was after him.

In the underground room the others were now recovering. The only one still unable to stand was A. B. Fox, who had not only been stunned by Hateman and thrown down the steps but had breathed in a lot of the sleeping gas.

Uncle carried him up the steps and laid him on the grass in the fresh air, giving him a dose of Gleamhound's Faintness Producer for Enemies, and he sat up at once.

Sure of Fox's recovery, Uncle looked round on the Crack House enclosure like a general viewing his army. The Badfort crowd were not just being allowed to escape, but were once more being driven round and round by his infuriated followers. There was Waldovenison Smeare with an old chair-leg, Snowjuice with a broom and Mrs Snowjuice with a toasting-fork. Woeband was chasing Jellytussle and syringeing him with pond water. He hates getting wet, for his jelly melts. Even Tabby Bismuth had seized a prickly branch of miserberry bush, and was beating Hitmouse who was entangled in the rubber coils and cylinders of his gas-pumping machine, so that he couldn't escape. He was being badly pricked and scratched, and was blubbering hideously at the bottom of a trench. Every time he reached for a skewer he received another blow from the miserberry branch.

Hateman was more shaken than he had ever been, for Uncle's blow with the club had caught him with such force that he couldn't walk straight. He was last seen limping through the narrow passage that led to Gaby's Marsh.

The fight seemed to be won, and Uncle was beginning to relax when he saw a hideous, bat-like shape gliding down over the tops of the towers.

"Look out, Leominster!" roared Uncle. "Batty's back!"

Those who saw it were never to forget the encounter between the atrocious Batty and Leominster.

"You vile fizz-merchant!" he screamed at Uncle as he alighted on the grass, his terrifying fists clenched, his lilac eyes blazing. "You money-goat! You turkey-snatcher! You poor-man's-penny-thief!"

Uncle started across the grass determined to deal finally with the wretched creature, but Leominster was before him.

With splendidly tossing mane and a roar that echoed like thunder among the towers, the massive lion was upon Batty, and he was flung a tangled mass of torn wings, bruised fists, and black eyes into the pond.

The ducks fled for their lives. Their quacking added to the noise made by the hideous bubbling and screaming of Batty, and by Leominster's tremendous roars.

No wonder that Uncle's party, creeping palely out from Crack House into the fresh air, looked about them with dazed eyes.

Cloutman and Gubbins were terribly distressed. They think of themselves as being Uncle's strong-arm men, and now a battle had been fought without their aid while they lay helpless.

"Cheer up," said Uncle. "There will be other fights! That you can be sure of!"

Now that the One-Armed Badger had recovered he was extremely happy, for his first-aid box was in great demand and he had thoughtfully brought a big bottle of Hot Joey. This liquid, mixed with boiling water, makes a splendid drink for exhausted people, and Mrs Snowjuice and Tabby Bismuth were soon handing round steaming mugs. Smoothy sent for a strengthening supply of Pigweed Truffle Buns and Seaweed Slashers, and they all felt happy as they sat on the grass recovering. They felt a great danger had been averted and that Crack House was free from the terror that had haunted it for so long.

NINETEEN

Peace and Presents

THE next day dawned bright and clear. After the horrible events in the underground room Uncle and the Old Monkey felt it was good to stand outside the front door of Homeward and enjoy the sunshine and fresh air.

As they were doing so a large car drove over the drawbridge. It was rather shabby, but it had a gold crown on the bonnet.

It was the state vehicle of the King of the Badgers.

The monarch stepped out, came up the steps and said to Uncle:

"Congratulations on a splendid victory, sir. It surpasses all your others, and my people wish to express their gratitude and make a small presentation."

"Thank you, your Majesty," said Uncle. "It is very good of them, but I intend to call this a day of Peace and Presents, and the presentation to everybody is to come from myself this time. This includes yourself if you can stoop to accept it. I suppose your Majesty would not object to a personal gift of cash for once?"

Many, many times has the needy King called on Uncle for help, so this was a polite way of putting it. The King replied in the same dignified way:

"No, sir. Under the circumstances I should be pleased to accept a gift of coin from you, but in private, please."

"I have already taken steps with this in view," said Uncle, and signalled to the Old Monkey. "Earlier this morning I visited my treasury."

The King's eyes gleamed with hope. He is very hard-pressed for money most of the time.

The Old Monkey wheeled up a large sack on a barrow. Nobody else knew what was in it, but Uncle has few secrets from the Old Monkey.

"In that sack," said Uncle, "you will find notes and coin to the value of about £100,000. I haven't had time to count it properly, but will that be of use?"

"Use!" whispered the King of the Badgers. "It will set me on my feet and help me to reduce the rates which I feel are too high!"

"Good!" said Uncle. "We need say no more. Now my idea of the day is this. No floral decorations. The castle will, of course, have a few flags out and electric lights from top to bottom, and the great searchlight will be working on Captain Walrus's lighthouse. After refreshments I will make a short speech of about five minutes, and everybody will be pleased and somewhat enriched when they hear it. If your Majesty will do me the favour of seeing that this gathering is announced, it will help me. Let all come about two this afternoon, and they will hear something that will do them good."

The King promised to do this and drove off much happier than when he had arrived.

Smoothy, who had been spending the night at Homeward, had a short conference about the gold block with Uncle while he finished off a couple of Seaweed Slashers.

"We'll have to think of the gold block as a gold reserve; lots of great countries have one," said Uncle. "It means that everybody knows we can pay our way. What d'you say to that?"

"Big responsibility," said Smoothy, "but it's the only way. The Badfort crowd will try to get at it, but if Cowgill's defences are good they won't succeed. Anyway, we can perhaps think out a scheme or two for using part of it from time to time."

"Yes, for the general good," said Uncle. "That needs discussing. I've taken a fancy to your great greenhouse, Smoothy. I intend to spend a number of days there munching, swimming, wallowing – and planning."

"Suits me," said Smoothy, "and tell Cowgill to get cracking with the fence. I don't want Whitebeard sleeping on the gold block, guarding it for ever."

And that was how the matter was left for the time.

The message from the King of the Badgers spread rapidly, and long before two o'clock the whole area of Homeward was crowded with all sorts of people, animals and birds. They brought singers, bands, clowns and other performers, and even lit fires to add a festive look to the scene.

At two thirty Uncle, with the King of the Badgers, Smoothy, Waldovenison Smeare and his own close friends, came out on to a platform that Cowgill had hurriedly erected in front of Homeward so that Uncle could clearly be seen by all.

The King of the Badgers spoke first and a fanfare of one hundred trumpets sounded to announce him.

"Friends," he began, "today our host calls a day of Peace and Presents, and what could be better! He insists that no token should come from us, but for once I must disagree with our great benefactor. I hope he will not be displeased with me, but I have commissioned our most distinguished artist, Mr Waldovenison Smeare, to execute a vast mural here at Homeward, depicting the life and deeds of the owner of the castle. It will be about 100 feet long by 30 feet high, so Mr Smeare will be occupied for months. What do you say, my friends?"

The following cheers, given by so many animals with different voices, made an almost bewildering tornado of noise, but at last there was stillness and Uncle spoke:

"Friends, you know I don't like long speeches, so I will just say thank you for the promise of the great mural. I shall watch its progress with keen interest, and when it is finished we must have another celebration."

A brass band began to play, 'Hail to Glorious Uncle'.

Also a band of young badgers began to sing the well-known song which begins:

"We love to hear of Uncle's deeds;
He makes us feel so glad;
His bounty makes the poor man rich
And fills with joy the sad.

"How vast his stores of ham and lard;
How huge his vats of oil ... "

Unfortunately they had only got as far as this when an atrocious raucous voice away on the edge of the crowd interrupted them:

"See that pompous humbug Unc
On the platform raise his trunk ... "

Somebody instantly stopped whoever it was, but the incident was sordid and unfortunate. Uncle felt the only dignified course was to take no notice of it.

"Now, friends, I wish to tell you that recently," he continued, "there has been discovered on Mr Smoothy's property within the walls of my castle a great mass of gold. He and I have discussed at length how best to use it for the general good. At first we thought of coining gold pieces and giving them away, but financial experts have warned us that prices would rise and nobody would be better off. So, as you are all my tenants, we have decided that when you come to pay your weekly rent we will give you each a shilling whatever rent you pay. That means that at the end of the year you will have received more than twice as much as if I had given you a golden pound today. But some will need a little ready cash to celebrate the occasion, so Mr Smoothy and I have made preparations so that each of you, as you pass over the drawbridge on the way home, will receive a new half-crown. That is all. You will find plenty of provisions, so eat as much as you want and be happy."

Again the applause was so deafening that a vast crowd of herons rose startled into the sky, and were joined by many blackbirds, thrushes and larks who find the easiest way to cheer is to fly swiftly to and fro.

A few people were disappointed at not getting a pound down, but when they thought it out they decided that this way of distributing the money was best.

In fact all were pleased except the Badfort crowd. As the interruption with the song showed, a number of them were hanging about, as usual, on the edges of the crowds, trying to pick up what they could.

Hateman, who was still limping a little, was there with Hitmouse, who still showed some of the scratches of the miserberry attack. Hitmouse was writing in his hating book, and trying to stick skewers into people whenever he could.

"Rotten idea!" muttered Hateman. "It will be fearfully hard work robbing people of these beggarly half-crowns, but we must do our best. Meanwhile let's swallow as much as we can of the free food!"

Five minutes after this he snatched a tin of Python Whiffets from a small refreshment stall set up by Colonel Lungy. This kind old man was determined to repay Uncle for the rescue of his pedigree stock and the unmasking of Hateman by providing, as one of the attractions for Uncle's visitors, a taste of Eastern delicacies. Happily Juba Jelly was the main treat, and small plates of this beautiful delicacy were given for all winners in the games of Cheese Spigots, Orange-and-Lemon Cricket, and Christmas Pudding Football. As Colonel Lungy was so busy serving out this extremely exclusive jelly, he had no time to tell long stories, so the refreshment stall was a great success.

As darkness fell, the lights came out on all the various towers and the glamour of the evening was complete.

From the platform Uncle, at last, gave one short speech of farewell.

"Goodbye, friends," he said, "and thank you for all your good wishes and support. There are two people I must mention before you go. First there is my faithful friend, the One-Armed Badger, who thought of the best way for all to have a share in the treasure. He is too modest to appear, but if you look at this pile of parcels and goods at my side he is underneath it."

Everybody clapped and cheered, and looked with interest at the towering pile of packages which quivered a little as Uncle spoke.

"And also," continued Uncle, "I must mention the brilliant work of my detective A. B Fox."

Crashing cheers and whistles came from all sides, and A. B. Fox, who had a large piece of sticking plaster over one eye, bowed low and waved his magnificent brush in a stately arc of acknowledgement.

"I can only describe as staggering the way Mr Fox, faced with a baffling mystery, has *nosed* things out!"

More cheers and laughter. To Fox discoveries are all in the day's work, and he never shows his feelings very much; but even he seemed pleased by the general enthusiasm.

Gradually the great crowd melted away. Cowgill and Will Shudder distributed the half-crowns at the entrance to the drawbridge, and Cloutman and Gubbins stood near by in case of trouble.

That night, as Uncle and his friends were having a quietly cheerful evening around the fire in the hall of Homeward, Will Shudder turned on the radio.

Everybody was appalled to hear the following disgraceful interview being broadcast between Beaver Hateman and Hitmouse:

HITMOUSE (*thin and squeaky*). You were present at the vast gathering outside the Castle of Homeward today, Mr Hateman.

HATEMAN (*loud and raucous*). I watched what went on, you might say.

HITMOUSE. And what did you think of it, Mr Hateman?

HATEMAN. Hundreds Honour Humbug! That's what I thought!

HITMOUSE. Strong words, Mr Hateman. What are your opinions about the discovery of the gold block?

HATEMAN (*shouting*). Radio would bust if I said what I thought! Enough boodle there to do us all a bit of good, but what do the Arch Humbug and Pigweed Smoothy do with it? Keep it to themselves – that's what!

HITMOUSE. I thought every person in the land was given 2s. 6d. with promise of more to follow?

HATEMAN. More to follow. You've said it. A shilling every time the rent is paid. No rent, no shilling. That's what it amounts to! Bully Bounty knows most of the inhabitants of Homeward *don't pay rent*. Why should they? Now he's thought of a way of making them do it. A nice Lord Bountiful he is. And now I must give a warning in the name of humanity. If any listener was given a tin of Python Whiffets as a so-called reward, listen to your friend Beaver Hateman, B.A. Don't eat the whiffets, my friend; the arch poisoner of Homeward must be foiled. Leave them alone.

"Turn it off!" said Uncle. "Let's have a game of spigots. Pass the Koolvat and bring in a new bunch of bananas. Let's have a quiet festive evening, and tomorrow will look after itself."